DISSENSION

Chronicles of the Uprising: 1

K.A. Salidas

Cover Layout by Covers By Christian www.coversbychristian.com
Interior Layout by Katie Salidas http://www.katiesalidas.com
Editing by Sharazade

Published by:
Rising Sign Books
http://www.risingsignbooks.net

For more information about my books email:
katiesalidas@gmail.com

CHRONICLES OF THE UPRISING

Dissension - The great cataclysm wiped almost all life from the face of planet Earth, but tiny pockets of survivors crawled from the ashes, with only one thought: survival, at any cost.
But not all survivors were human.

In the dark, militant society that has risen in the aftermath, vampires, once thought to be mythical, have been assimilated and enslaved. Used for blood sport their lives are allowed to continue only for the entertainment of the masses. Reviled as savages, they are destined to serve out their immortal lives in the arena, as gladiators.

And there is no greater gladiator than Mira: undefeated, uncompromising...and seemingly unbreakable. When an escape attempt leads Mira into the path of Lucian Stavros, the city's Regent, her destiny is changed forever.

Lucian, raised in a culture which both reviles and celebrates the savagery and inhumanity of vampires, finds Mira as intriguing as she is brash. An impulsive decision - to become Mira's patron – changes more than just Lucian's perception about vampire kind. The course of his life is altered in ways he could never have predicted – a life that is suddenly as expendable as hers.

Can Mira prove to Lucian that all is not as it seems? Can Lucian escape centuries of lies, bloodshed, and propaganda to see the truth? Or will the supreme power of the human overlords destroy them both?

Complication - Narrowly escaping death at the hands of the Magistrate, Mira travels west, toward the coast. With three weakened human fugitives accompanying her, she searches for the mythical land of Sanctuary.

After encountering a pack of wolf shifters, headed by the charismatic—and brazen—Stryker, Mira learns that Sanctuary is real after all. Caldera Grove: home of the Otherkin. Hidden in the mouth of a dormant volcano, it has protected its residents from humans since the early days following the great cataclysm. For Mira— a vampire— Caldera Grove is a land of peace; an escape from the relentless persecution of the humans who once enslaved her, and an end to the daily struggle and bloodshed of being a gladiator.

For the humans accompanying her, Caldera Grove means death. Humans, greedy and untrustworthy creatures, are destroyed before they can penetrate its borders.

To plead her case for entry into Caldera, Mira must abandon her companions, albeit temporarily, and follow Stryker into the heart of the city. What she finds within Caldera Grove presents her with an unenviable decision between her own desires for freedom and peace, or honor and the human companions who risked it all for her.

Revolution - Peace is an illusion. Blood, violence, and death follow Mira like shadows.

Battle lines have been drawn between human and Otherkin, and a bloody war is on the horizon: one that will end in either a shift in the world's balance of power...or ultimate destruction.

In spite of their strength, powers, and a rage known only by the oppressed, the Otherkin are evenly matched by the superior numbers of the human army. To tip the balance in their favor, the Otherkin need more soldiers – and their only options are the Gladiators of New Haven city.

Mira is sent across enemy lines to recruit any able-bodied vampires to her cause. But what she discovers along the way will blur the lines between friends and enemies. Seeds of doubt weaken Mira's allegiance, and she finds herself torn between the old masters who used her as entertainment and the new ones who consider her as nothing more than a weapon.

As the war draws near, Mira will have to decide what she is truly fighting for.

Transition - Peace is just a breath between battles for Mira. Hardened by slavery and war, she longs for the simpler life, knowing that it might never be hers to enjoy. There is always another battle waiting to be fought, another foe on the horizon. Peace between humans, vampires, and otherkin may be nothing more than a dream, but Mira holds out hope. It is during this brief respite that Mira is gifted one of her greatest weapons. Though it brings with it memories of a time when she was not so jaded, it also comes with a reminder of terrible pain and loss. Awakening deeply hidden emotions within her, if Mira can use this to her advantage, she'll have a new ally in the next battle to come.

**More Titles planned. For more information visit
www.KatieSalidas.com**

For my sweet baby girl, Zoey.
I hope you grow up to be as strong as Mira.
Just don't be as jaded.

PROLOGUE

E veryone joked about the end of the world, but when it finally happened, no one was laughing.

December 21, 2012.

Mankind's final day had been predicted for years, but no one had believed it would ever come. Why would they? There had been so many dates labeled "the end," and none had yet come to pass.

When the sun rose on that fateful day, everyone made their little jokes. Just one more hoax. Street merchants started selling "I survived the apocalypse... again" T-shirts. Everybody looked around, shrugged their shoulders, and got back to what they'd been doing. The world moved on.

But the day starts at different times across the globe. This particular prophesy — this doomsday prediction — had been made by the Mayan people. It wasn't until the sun rose in South America that the destruction began.

Previously docile fault lines began to quake. As if waking from a slumber, the earth rumbled from deep within like some ravenous beast scenting its prey, to be satisfied only by utter annihilation.

Volcanoes that had lain dormant for hundreds of years suddenly sprang into action, erupting with centuries of pent-up pressure, spewing hot geysers of acrid smoke. Rivers of magma belched out from the mouths of these angry mountains, scorching the land and devouring everything caught in their deadly flow. Thick clouds blanketed the sky, choking out the sunlight. Searing chunks of pumice rained down upon the land, burying entire cities and all their occupants in a rocky grave.

For decades — centuries, even — the Earth had been beaten and bruised, scratched and bitten by her inhabitants. It was only natural that she would fight back. And her retribution was merciless. Whole continents fragmented as fault lines deepened and separated. The surface of the earth ripped apart while its terrified inhabitants futilely attempted to escape the destruction. Nowhere was safe. Giant waves of destruction beat down upon every coast, swallowing islands whole and obliterating coastal cities on mainlands. Never before had the loss of life been so devastating.

No one was laughing now.

It was truly, utterly, the end of days.

In the aftermath, the few that remained alive were forced to band together for survival. Food was scarce; shelter was even harder to come by. People who had never conceived of a life without electricity, running water, and fast food were faced with the ultimate choice: to live, by whatever means possible... or to die.

In the ragged days that followed the destruction, many more lives were lost — or taken — in the name of survival. Those who remained were few and far between.

And not all survivors were human.

Supernatural creatures — vampires — once thought to be the stuff of myth and legend, were forced from the refuge of the shadows. With no place left to hide, their only choice for survival was to reveal themselves to those few humans who remained. Immortality gave vampires the ability to weather the storms, but their weakness to sunlight left them vulnerable and in desperate need of shelter and protection during the harsh days following the great cataclysms. Only through collaboration could both races stand the slightest chance for survival.

It was an uneasy truce at first. The vampires' need for blood, no matter how small a dose, made them objects of hatred rather than companionship; but their ability to protect the former city-dwelling humans against other predators in the night counted greatly in their favor. Eventually, human and vampire learned to co-exist.

Slowly, as they always do, humans adapted to their newly reshaped home. Society rebuilt itself. Life continued on planet Earth and even began to flourish. Over the next hundred years, eight thriving cities rose from the ashes, and humans once again took their place as masters of the Earth.

And with that power came hubris.

Formerly friends and vital allies, the vampires quickly became targets – victims of the humans' drive to be top of the food chain. Rumors and lies spread quickly about what vicious and cold-hearted demons the vampires truly were. Human deaths, even when the cause was not loss of blood, were blamed on vampires. Long forgotten was the help the vampires had given to their human brethren in those early days of reconstruction.

The human race came to see vampires as nothing more than criminals and outlaws. Vermin. Using the vampires' vulnerability to sunlight and starvation, the humans turned their once-helpful protectors into slaves. Hunted down and brought to so-called justice, vampires were faced with the same brutal choice the humans had confronted a century earlier: Succumb to the will of humans, or end their days on Earth.

To live by whatever means possible… or to die.

CHAPTER ONE

April 17th, 2210 – New Haven City. *Westernmost* Province of the Iron Gate, Pacific Coast

The roar of the crowd, all twenty-five-thousand people in attendance, rose to a thundering crescendo when Mira delivered a bone-crunching blow to her opponent's ribs. Standing only five feet tall, she might not have appeared a formidable warrior, but the thin, spiky-haired waif of a vampire could hold her weight and more when put to the test. Amplified by the superb acoustics, the sound of bones cracking echoed through the Superdome arena. The defeated, a red-headed male vampire staggered, punch-drunk, and then dropped to his knees. Dirt and sweat coated his face but could not mask the fear in his icy blue eyes. His was a look Mira had seen so many times before. Her opponent's immortal life had finally come to an end, and he was ready to take the final deadly blow.

Above her, Mira knew the fifty-foot mega screen showed her hapless victim in brilliant resolution, ensuring that all who were attending, and those watching from the comfort of their homes, could see these last gruesome moments in crystal clear high-definition.

Mira gazed down at her opponent's blood-soaked face. Though he was her enemy for the moment, she did not relish having to end him. No one should be forced into the arena and told to kill or be killed. It wasn't right. But it was what was demanded of her, and given the choice between her life and someone else's… well, there really was no choice. No matter the cost, Mira was a survivor.

She glanced up to the large private box overlooking the arena. A well-dressed man in deep-purple robes sat, enjoying what appeared to be a dinner of filet mignon and roast potatoes. Even here, in the dusty arena below, Mira's enhanced senses picked up the tantalizing scent of very rare, bloody steak. She could hardly believe that a human could not only watch the murder about to take place, but also sit and eat the dead flesh of a once-living being while doing it. From the smell of it, the poor beast was practically still bleeding on his plate. Who was truly the more savage creature?

Over the crowd's roar, an announcer introduced the well-dressed man, Lucian Stavros, Regent of the Iron Gate. Lucian gently and purposefully slowly set down his knife and fork. He took another moment to wipe his face clean and then smiled, acknowledging the roaring crowd.

Chants of "Death, death, death" rang out from the throng as a single unified demand.

The Regent listened for a moment, making a show of putting his hands to his ears to hear screaming hoard's request, and then held a hand out, with his thumb pointed to the side.

As if the next moment were the most important, the anticipating mass hushed. Eerie silence filled the arena as everyone watched for the Regent to make his decision.

From her vantage point below, Mira saw the steely look of determination cross the Regent's face. If she didn't know better, she might have thought he took this decision seriously; but then, he was human, and they never cared much if her kind lived or died. Lucian Stavros took a cursory glance down at Mira. Their eyes met. It was only a brief moment, but in that short time, Mira saw him waver.

Could it be true, she wondered, or was it just a trick of the light? No human actually cared about the lives of vampires. The moment faded, and the fleeting thought left.

Mira saw the Regent's decision. He turned his thumb down. Death!

The crowd went wild.

The last hope for her defeated opponent had vanished; Mira had to finish him. "Sorry," she whispered to the half-dead vampire on his knees before her. Though her fangs tingled at the prospect of tasting his final dying moments — her reward, if you could call it that, for living through another battle — she did not enjoy what she was about to do. Like her, he was a slave, forced into servitude to the humans as they saw fit. He had not asked for this, and neither had she. But, despite what either of them wanted, it was the will of the crowd, the humans, that had to be served.

Aiming to sever the carotid artery with her fangs, Mira dove at her opponent's neck. His death would be quick. At least she could afford him that luxury.

Hot, sweet, and energizing, his blood flowed freely down her parched throat. She'd been starved for so long. Denied the one thing she needed. And now, free to drink her fill, it was all she could do not to let the beast within her take over. Blood was everything: food, drink, life-giving essence, and pure ecstasy. Even the smallest amount could provide healing nourishment and pleasure all at once. But Mira could not let herself take pleasure from it, knowing the source. This was no willing donor. This was a fallen comrade. A fellow vampire. One of her own kind. His death ordered by the command of the humans. No matter how good his blood tasted, it was not for her to enjoy. She'd take only what she needed to heal from her wounds, and let his death come quickly.

More cheers erupted around Mira. The crowd, despite being entirely human, proved more bloodthirsty than she. The irony of it was sickening. Distantly, she heard the announcer proclaim her the winner.

With a roar, she threw her head back, ripping out her opponent's throat, spraying what remained of his blood out into the air. They wanted carnage – they could have it. She had to keep her adoring fans happy lest they turn on her. In the arena, the life or death of a gladiator often came down to the will of the crowd. And though she was repulsed by what she had to do, she knew how to play the game.

The satisfying flush of fresh blood in her system and the heady rush that came with it was short lived. The reality of her situation was always close to the surface. Above, the giant dome roof parted, sending a hot blast of UV light down around Mira like a cage.

Not wanting to let them regain their strength, the humans were quick to remind vampires where their place was and who their masters were. Not even afforded a moment's respite for her victory, Mira was already enduring the painful reminder that she was a slave. Worse, a prisoner.

Her skin singed where the light touched. Instinctively, she held up her hands in surrender. The faster she let them haul her away to the prison level, the better.

The crowd around still roared with applause. But were they cheering for Mira, or happy to see her being tortured by blinding light? A bit of both, probably. Humans loved to see any bit of vampire suffering. Though it angered her, Mira would not show it and invite their ire.

Two humans, one male and one female, approached Mira, both wearing standard issue black Kevlar body suits and hoods with a wooden stake and hammer emblazoned across the chest. Handlers. Specially trained to deal with vampires and equipped to kill if necessary. Among their weapons were UV torches, quick blasting light sticks able to direct a powerful beam of ultraviolet light at the push of a button. The female's hand inched towards her UV torch as they approached Mira. She was a new appointee as Mira's handler, who preferred to shoot first and ask questions later. Mira hated the mocha-skinned Amazon wannabe and would have loved nothing more than to rip her to shreds. Few females were allowed to be handlers, and this one had wanted to prove herself from the moment she'd been assigned to Mira.

Once Mira might have acted on her desire to kill the nuisance handler and take whatever punishment she'd be given, but after years in this prison Mira had learned her lesson. Fighting back was best done strategically. Immortality was not invincibility, and she was no fool.

"Arms out, slave." The largest of the two handlers, a male with a deep voice, barked the order at her.

"Come to congratulate me on my victory and adorn me with jewelry?" With a cocky smile, she held out her hands, awaiting the silver cuffs with which they'd restrain her.

"Silence!" The male refused to look at her. He fastened the cuffs around her wrists and pulled back quickly, almost as if he feared what Mira might do.

Silver stung her skin, but Mira wouldn't let on that she was in any pain. "I always did have a thing for the strong silent types." She smirked despite the discomfort the cuffs were already creating. Hives were beginning to pepper Mira's smooth alabaster skin. An annoying allergic reaction, but she'd never admit how much it bothered her. Any sign of weakness could be exploited.

The male handler refused to acknowledge her or engage her further. He continued to work shackling her feet and then connected another silver chain between the two sets of restraints. When finished, he pointed toward the door at the edge of the arena. The female handler pressed a few buttons on a small communicator device around her wrist. Above, the dome began to close, and the shafts of light surrounding Mira vanished.

Thankful to be back in the dark, Mira nodded to her handlers as if to say, "Lead on," and followed as they directed her away from the arena, down to the pens.

Her moment of fame was over.

CHAPTER TWO

Not a word was exchanged between **Mira** and her handlers as they exited the arena and headed down through the lower levels toward the prison. Only the sound of their bootsteps on the smooth concrete broke the silence. Not that Mira had anything to say to the pair of humans who ushered her back and forth from the arena to her cell, but it would be nice if occasionally she was treated as something more than an unwanted creature whose usefulness had ended the moment she dealt her final blow in the arena.

The silence ended as they passed through a set of thick metal doors. The light beyond dimmed, but the echoes of agony through the corridors became intensely vivid. Deep within the underground, where no sunlight could reach, was where the vampires were kept. Dark and dank, scented with the foul odor of unwashed bodies, blood, and mold, this was the place Mira called home, the only place she'd known for the last thirty years. She was lucky to have lived that long. Countless other vampires had come and gone before her, and many more had been slain at the point of her own teeth. The gladiator's life was all she knew now. Occasionally there were vague remembrances of what life had been like before her capture, but almost her entire vampire existence had been down in these dirty cells.

Fed only with the blood of other unwanted vermin, the humans had practically starved Mira and her kind to the point of savagery. It not only served to keep her kind more eager to fight in the arena, but also reinforced the image of their savagery in the human population's mind.

Rounding one dark corridor and heading down another equally gloomy one, the trio traveled further into the murky underbelly of the arena. Mournful howls and agonizing screams grated on Mira's nerves as they passed by the Hall of Punishment. Vampires who failed in battle but had not been killed were made to suffer unthinkable tortures at the hands of their human owners. Mira had unfortunately seen the inside of that hall on more than one occasion. If vampires could scar, she'd be unrecognizably disfigured from her time within those walls. Her punishments, rather than for failure in battle, had been ordered as attempts to break her spirit. No one, neither her handlers nor her Owner, had any affection for Mira. Free-spirited, uncooperative, and cocky as she was, Mira had not broken. Not once. No matter what vile punishments they'd thrown at her. As long as she was imprisoned in Iron Gate, she had one thought and one thought only… freedom. She'd have it someday, no matter how long it took. But though she loathed the arena and the life she had to lead, she knew that staying alive was the only way to get that freedom she so desired. And to do that, she had to remain a winner in the arena. It was the only reason she was still alive, despite her many attempts at escape and even more episodes of bad behavior. She knew as long as she kept winning, and earning her Owner lots of prize money, she'd be safe from final death.

They passed through a large corridor of prison cells before finally reaching Mira's, a small six-by-eight-foot cage of silver-coated steel bars with an automatically locking doorway. Her door, marked number 8254-A, was locked via an electronic keypad. Mira casually glanced over, trying to be as inconspicuous as possible, as they entered the ten-digit access code on the keypad. 753951…

The butt of a UV torch connected with the back of her head. A lightning fast jolt of pain had Mira hissing through gritted teeth.

"Eyes forward, slave," the female handler ordered.

Instinct more than anger drove Mira to turn on her handler. The fresh throbbing in her head mixed with frantic energy from her recent feed. Mira snarled, fangs bared, ready to strike, and advanced on the female handler.

Gone was the stony expression on the human woman's face. Fear widened her eyes. Realization. Complete understanding of what a vampire is capable of, especially a formidable arena gladiator who'd just fed...

"Stand down, vampire." The human woman tried to put authority into her voice, but her fear was clear, and Mira wasn't in the mood to take orders.

With little effort, Mira snapped apart the silver shackles and grabbed hold of her handler's neck. Ready to squeeze the human woman like a bug, Mira tightened her grip, choking off the handler's air supply as she forced her backwards onto the silver-coated cell bars.

Alarms sounded all around her. The other handler turned on his UV light and shined it in Mira's face. She closed her eyes against the sting but refused to let go. Fangs still bared, she bit blindly at her handler, enjoying the terrified screams, savoring the delicious tremors running through the human's weak body.

An army of heavy-footed steps flooded the corridor. More handlers were arriving. Mira had shaken up the hornets' nest this time. The taste of the handler's fresh blood would not be worth the punishment they'd deliver if she killed the human. Just as she was ready to release her prey, the entire cell block flooded with light. In a fraction of a second, Mira's skin felt as if it had gone up in flames. She, however, was not the only one to suffer. Other vampires peacefully lounging in their cells began to howl in pain as the dreadful light filled every inch of space.

Her whole body on fire, Mira released her prey and balled herself up, trying to hide in the small shadows created by those standing around her.

Something hard connected with Mira's head. She blacked out for the briefest of moments, which was all the humans needed to shove her into her cell and slam the door shut. Once secured, the lights went out and an eerie silence replaced the previous chaos.

"Try that again, you fucking leech, and we'll see you staked out in the morning sun," the male handler spat at her. He held tight to his compatriot, inspecting her Kevlar suit for any signs of damage.

Skin crispy, flaking off of her body, there wasn't an inch of Mira that didn't hurt; yet still she managed to laugh. "Come in here and say that, big man."

The male handler, having finished his once-over of his partner, turned his UV torch on Mira in response.

Already at the limits of what she could feel, Mira continued to laugh through the burning blast of light.

"She's fucking crazy," the female handler yelled over Mira's cackling laughter.

The male handler nodded stiffly and clicked off his torch. "What do you expect, she's a leech."

"Yeah, because humans are so sane," Mira retorted. Though she tried to sound cocky, she couldn't hide the edge of pain in her voice. There was not an inch of her body that was not raw and angry at that moment.

"Don't let her taunt you. File an incident report on that crazy leech, and she'll get what's coming to her." The voices trailed off.

Mira stared up at the ceiling. The coolness of the concrete floor was a small comfort to her searing skin. Her wounds were already beginning to heal, thanks to the blood she'd been able to drink in battle, but Mira knew that was the last she'd taste for a while. No doubt the handlers would report her to her Owner, and she'd be given some archaic punishment for her crimes. Even in their heyday, vampires had never been as cruel as the humans now were to them. Some deserved death, sure, but the rest just wanted to live their eternity in comfort and peace.

"Good job, Mira," George, a male vampire in the adjacent cell groaned. "Did we all need to suffer for your midnight snack?"

Mira huffed in frustration, at war with herself over what she'd just done. Part of her felt guilty for what the other vampires had endured because of her actions, but another part was not going to stand by idly while the humans attacked her for no reason. "You're just jealous because you don't have the balls to try it yourself."

"I'm not that stupid." George's dark bald head appeared at the bars. Though he sounded angry, none of it showed in his concerned expression. "This is a maximum security facility. There are cameras, monitors, sensors. Face it, honey, we're stuck in here until the day we die."

"Well, as I recall, you were the one doing the fucking last night. You were gone more than five hours." Her muscles protested every movement, but Mira slowly rolled over on to her stomach and gingerly pushed herself up to her knees. She was healing, but not quickly enough for her liking. "Is it true? Did you get a new Patron?"

"I know how to play the game." A cocky smile replaced the look of concern. George flashed her his perfectly white, perfectly sharp teeth. Tall, well-built, dark skinned-for a vampire – and that beautiful bald head human women seemed to just adore. That man knew his strengths; he was a handsome devil who flaunted it every chance he got, and it worked wonders. He hadn't been in the arena for well over a month, too busy with his ever-growing list of admirers. "Yep. Got myself a hot vein and a little free time. Which is more than most of us can hope for."

"Well, have fun being a human's play toy," she grumbled. Jealousy burned in Mira's gut. She may not have been a tradition-al beauty, but she was the best fighter in the place, and she'd never attracted a Patron. Fresh blood. Small comforts. The ability to leave your cell, even if it was only to service your Patron. Those were luxuries she'd never been afforded. George was a pretty face, he wasn't even that great a fighter, and somehow he had managed to get Patrons lining up around the building for a few moments of his service.

"Oh, I will. Beats the punishment you're about to endure."

Mira lifted her head just enough to see a pair of expensive heels walking down the way toward her cell. She knew the familiar clip-clop of her Owner's stilettos. *Damn*. She'd hoped it would be a little while longer before her Owner had gotten wind of Mira's disobedience.

Speaking of traditional beauties... her Owner, a former runway model and a pretty little princess in her own right, seethed with anger as she approached the cell. Mira didn't need to look up to know the deep hazel eyes of Olivia Preston were staring down at her through impossibly long and thick eyelashes. Her perfectly pink lip would be curled upward in a dangerous sneer. Olivia was the worst kind of Owner Mira could have landed: beautiful, spoiled, and self-important. "Stand up, slave. Show your master some respect!"

Respect. The woman didn't know the meaning of the word. Olivia Preston was well known for treating everyone — vampire and human alike — as if they were her things. Try as she might, Mira could hardly hold back her contempt for the pampered little princess. "The fact that I haven't attempted to rip your throat out is a show of respect all its own."

Unaffected by Mira's threat, Olivia continued to stare down the imprisoned vampire. "If you weren't such a damn good fighter, I'd have you put down like the dog you are."

"I should be so lucky."

Olivia wouldn't follow through with that threat; Mira knew that, though she could do many worse things. She wouldn't kill her prize fighter. The money Mira earned her for all the battles she'd won had paid for every piece of expensive clothing she wore, all the way down to her gaudy, gem-encrusted heels.

"I had come here to congratulate you on your win today..."

Mira waited in silence, refusing to look up at her Owner, who was impatiently tapping her heels on the concrete ground. She knew there was nothing at the end of that sentence that she really wanted to hear.

Olivia's foot came to rest. "...Instead, I get a report you attacked your handler."

"She threw the first punch." Mira laughed. "Too bad she couldn't back it up." She shouldn't have said it, but couldn't hold her tongue.

"This was meant to be your reward."

Mira had to look up this time to see just what her Owner was holding.

Clutched in her pale pink claws, was a small vial with red liquid inside.

Instinctively, Mira began to salivate. Blood. As much as she enjoyed disrespecting her Owner, this might not have been the best time to do it.

Recognition flashed in Olivia's hazel eyes. "Yes. Now I have your attention, don't I?

She dropped the small vial to the ground, where it shattered.

The sweet scent of that crimson liquid wafted up to Mira's nose. *Such a terrible waste.* It almost brought a tear to her eyes. If she hadn't already fed today, she'd probably have licked it off the floor, shards of glass and all. Other vampires in the area had caught wind of the smell too, and they whined and begged for a small taste.

Olivia sneered at Mira. "You need an attitude adjustment. You want to smart off and be disrespectful to me… you'll pay for it."

Here it comes: the punishment. There was nothing for her to say; she'd already said enough to piss off her Owner.

"Forty-eight hours in the lightbox. No blood after. Perhaps that will teach you a little respect." She turned on her heel and stormed away.

"Respect. Ha! I haven't learned it yet. And you haven't earned it," Mira shouted back to her Owner. She was already in for the worst punishment possible – might as well get in a final jab while she could.

"Damn, girl." George whistled. "Humans do love a tan, but you're going to be one crispy thing after forty-eight hours."

Mira had no reply. He spoke the truth. The lightbox was truly the worst kind of punishment a vampire could be given. Intermittent flashes of light just long enough to burn but not long enough to kill. It was with methods like this that the humans had enslaved her kind. One weakness was all they needed to exploit. Humans grossly outnumbered vampires, and with this one weakness, they had brought the vampire nation to its knees.

CHAPTER THREE

Two **days of pure hell inside that tiny metal box** had fried more than Mira's skin. Anger boiled over inside her. At that moment she hated humans and everything about them. Worst of all, she hated the fact she had once been a human. To have anything in common with those savage inhumane beasts was an outrage. Weak and exhausted, Mira needed blood so badly she could barely walk, a fact that had her handlers noticeably on edge. A starving vampire could snap at any moment's time. Taking extra precautions, they used the thickest silver coated chains and cuffs possible. She'd also been fitted with a ball gag for the trek back to her cell. Even with the additional precautions, Mira could tell the female handler was nervous. There was no mistaking the tang of fear in the air. Still, though she was clearly still concerned about Mira's temperament, the female handler did not hold back her contempt as she roughly pulled Mira's lumbering and aching body towards the cell.

Just the simple act of putting one foot in front of the other was a laborious task. Every movement hurt, every muscle ached; her skin, burnt and raw, pulled and ripped with each movement. Wanting nothing more than a few moments of darkness and peace, Mira found the strength to lift her gaze long enough to watch the male handler's fingers nimbly tap the ten digit code into the lock pad. 95182… Before she could spy the last few numbers, her handler shifted his body in front, blocking her view. The pattern seemed simple enough that she might guess the next few numbers. When she was healthy enough, she'd try it. For now, she could barely hold herself upright. A rarity for her, Mira didn't even move as they undid her bonds. She welcomed their removal. One less pain in the sea of agony she was swimming in.

Like a sack of garbage, Mira was tossed down on the cold concrete floor. She hissed as her head came crashing down against the unyielding ground. Stars danced in her vision. They slammed the cell door shut behind her. The echo of the bars clanging together added to the sharpness of her aching head.

Every inch of Mira was raw and exposed. Her burned skin cracked and peeled. Nerves on edge, even the slightest flicker from the overhead lamp caused her to jump.

Damn them. Fucking humans.

"How was the tanning salon?" George taunted.

She was in no mood for his playful jabs, and feared opening her mouth because there was no telling what manner of verbal bile she might accidentally spew in his direction. Times like this, there was only one thing to soothe Mira's vicious spirit. She needed blood. Fast. Problem was, Mira couldn't remember if she'd stashed the last of her rations, or if she'd been too gluttonous the last time she'd been punished. Rations, even for her, a prize fighter, were few and far between. Every tiny drop was coveted, and occasionally, she overindulged. Mira hoped there would be something left over. Who knew when she'd be allowed to feed again? And in her current state, she was this close to losing all control.

"Seriously, girl, you all right?" All humor had left George's voice.

"Blood," Mira rasped, still trying to summon the energy to check her hiding spot, a small pocket she'd created inside her mattress sitting on the floor.

George's voice dropped to a whisper. "I got you, girl. Just give me a minute."

Not sure what he meant, Mira grunted, neither in agreement nor protest. Using all of her remaining energy, she rolled onto her back and closed her eyes, enjoying this brief moment of peace. In the cell next to hers, Mira heard George rumbling around in his cell.

"Had a little something stored up for a rainy day," he whispered, and Mira's mood lightened.

George to the rescue. As much as she was jealous of him for the easy lifestyle he had in comparison to hers, she was glad to count him as a friend. He had a good heart, offering to share his blood rations with her. That quality was extremely rare among the other vampires. Caged as they all were, most had reverted to animalistic creatures, embodying the savage image the humans wanted everyone to believe rather than remaining the once-proud vampires they had been. They'd just as easily kill you for the practice.

George tapped on the cell bars. Mira's eyes opened and she zeroed in on the small thing clutched in his hands.

"I'm going to roll it between the bars. You think you can grab it?"

Mira groaned in assent. She barely had the energy to keep her eyes open. Moving, rolling, anything involving actual muscles seemed almost impossible, but for blood, she'd have to try. She turned her head toward his cell and watched as he bent down low and released a small red vial. Salivating as if it were the last supper, she followed with her eyes as the small glass tube rolled toward her.

George stood and turned back to his mattress. "It's not much, but it will help."

With all her might, muscles screaming, she threw herself over, rolling on top of the vial as it came toward her. Not wanting any cameras to spot her with it, she rested her body over the small vial. Gingerly, she moved, every motion pulling away loose scales of burned flesh. The full-body pain was beyond measure, but still she pressed on, lifting her arm, moving her hand over the vial. Still hovering over it, she unscrewed the cap and palmed it her hand. The scent of it was intoxicating, even stale as it was. The moment the scent hit her nose, it was all she could think of. Pretending to have a coughing fit, Mira brought the vial to her lips. The first drop of old rat's blood hit her tongue. Thick and gelatinous as it was, it still tasted like heaven. Her parched throat burned for more, but after only a few mouthfuls the tiny vial was empty.

The effect was immediate: Her skin began to tingle, and wounds started to knit themselves together. Healing had always been a vampire's best gift. Given just a little blood, the renewal and repair happened within minutes. Raw, angry burns cooled and the pain slowly receded from her head. Looking more like her old self, but still not quite feeling it, Mira attempted very clumsily to stand. She was too wobbly to make it the first time, but at least her voice had returned.

"Thanks," she said earnestly to George. His act of kindness would not go unrewarded. She'd make sure of that somehow.

"I'm just glad to help a fellow vamp out. We got to stick together." George waved a dismissive hand and relaxed back onto his mattress. "You'd have done the same for me, girl."

"Probably."

"Oh, don't act all tough. I know you got my back." George's playful tone had returned now that it appeared everything was okay with Mira.

Testing her legs, Mira attempted again to stand, but her muscles had not yet regained their strength, and she collapsed back on the ground.

"Take it easy, girl." George propped himself up on his elbows and stared into Mira's cell. Their eyes met for a moment while Mira struggled to move. "You don't have to always be so tough."

"Weakness gets you killed." Mira pushed harder, and brought herself up on both legs. "And I'm not weak." She held tight to the silver-coated bars, using them for support. Even with the sting of the metal against her palms, she refused to let go and risk collapsing again.

"Your attitude is what's going to get you killed. Maybe you should try not to smart off to the handlers for a little? You know, there are rewards for good behavior."

"No."

"Somehow I knew you would say that." With an exasperated sigh, George flopped back onto his mattress.

"I can't change who I am any more than you can." Taking a moment to steady herself, she let go of the bars and took a slow but determined step toward her mattress.

"I know. I just hate seeing you go through all this time and time again because you give in to their taunting."

"I'd hardly call fighting back 'giving in,'" Mira snarled, appalled that George would even suggest that fighting for one's own self-respect was a bad thing. "Besides, I won't have to put up with any taunting for much longer."

"No. Not again, Mira." Fear sharpened George's tone. "No more plans. No more escape attempts. They're going to kill you the next time you get caught."

"I've got it all figured out this time." After a few successful baby steps, Mira felt confident she'd regained her strength and allowed herself to relax onto her mattress and rest.

"No. I'm not listening to you. You're going to get yourself killed."

"So. Be. It. I'm not a fucking animal, George. I'm a vampire. Remember what it was like to be free? To hunt? To enjoy the night? When was the last time you saw a full moon? Do you even remember?"

"Yeah, I remember, but in thirty years, I've never seen a vampire escape or earn their freedom, so you can forget about it." There was an odd finality in George's tone. Something Mira had never heard before. She decided to take the hint and drop the subject. She propped her head up on her pillow and stared up at the ceiling.

She'd been here for at least thirty years herself, though she couldn't be quite sure. Days and nights all blended together into one long blur of time. Freedom, though, and the smell of the fresh outdoors – those remained crystal clear in her memory. Sweet freedom. The simplicity and beauty of life before she'd been taken by the humans. Mira's heart yearned for just a small taste of that joy again.

George wasn't right. Just because no one had ever succeeded didn't mean she wouldn't find a way. She had to. Mira couldn't live the rest of her immortality locked here as a gladiator until the day she was killed in battle. She'd already lost so much; she would not give the humans the satisfaction of taking her life for entertainment purposes. She'd find a way, or die fighting for her freedom.

The pain, long since buried deep within her, resurfaced. Her last night of freedom had been the most painful. Memories came flooding back and tears rushed to Mira's eyes. She turned her face into the pillow so that no one would see.

No matter how hard she tried, she could not push away the memory. It played out moment by excruciating moment before her. A small cadre of vampires, Theo at the lead, had taken refuge in a rocky encampment outside the redwood forest, hoping to avoid the human patrol and wait out the day. The coast was still another evening's run, and if they hoped to flee the country, they'd have to make it to the Pacific Ocean.

Tears soaked through her pillow. That night had been the last time she had seen her lover alive. Theo. His deep green-brown eyes would haunt her dreams for the rest of eternity. Human soldiers invaded their campsite just before dawn.

She found her lover headless, his corpse drenched in his own blood.

It was the beginning of the end for her. Frozen where she stood, she hadn't even seen the soldier who had come up behind her. A silver-lined hood stole her vision, and the next thing Mira knew, she was being delivered to a Social Reassignment Facility. Vampire prison.

No fresh air. No beautiful moonlight. No freedom.

For weeks after, she endured unspeakable torture. The humans knew there was a vampire refuge somewhere, and they knew Mira had been heading for it. It was the only reason she'd been kept alive. But she would never betray her kind.

Having proven her strength and ability to take abuse, Mira was sold into the slave trade to be used as a gladiator. That had become her lot in this life: fight until the day she died her true and final death.

Footsteps echoed in the distance. A fast, heavy pace. Men. Handlers, most likely, here to bring round two of torture, no doubt. Mira dreaded the next round of her penance, but resigned herself to it. Couldn't be any worse than the lightbox.

"Prisoner 8254-B, stand and make yourself ready," the short, clipped male voice announced.

Relief escaped from Mira's mouth in a loud sigh. Weak as she still felt, and knowing her face was flushed with emotional tears, Mira was never more glad to not have her number called.

She listened to the sound of the keypad as the handler entered in the code for George's cell. Interestingly, his code was only eight numbers, whereas hers was ten. Were all the cells coded with not only different numbers but different lengths of code as well? She'd have to pay closer attention each time a vampire was pulled from their cell. Good information for future reference. George might argue against it, but for all he'd done for her, she'd find a way to get him out too. It was the least she could do.

A soft click confirmed the correct code, and then the cell door opened. Mira glanced over to her friend. The tall, bald vampire held his hands out willingly, ready to accept his shackles. George was always such a good boy. His eyes flitted over to her. "Be a good girl while I'm gone," he whispered.

"No talking," the handler barked at him, and then turned in Mira's direction. "And you, don't look so cocky. We'll be back for you in a moment. You've earned yourself extra training."

In an effort to appease George, Mira bit her tongue rather than respond to the handler's taunting.

Training – that was a funny way to describe it. Just as many vampires died in the training hall as in the arena. "No rest for the wicked," Mira sighed. She wished she'd had a little more blood to help gain her strength back.

CHAPTER FOUR

Harsh fluorescent lights glared down from high rafters. Mira hit the dirt-covered ground with a groan. Still weak from her time in the lightbox, her already screaming muscles threatened to give out, but she had to keep going. The six-foot-five vampire charging her was not about to stop. The only true difference between an arena battle and training was the size of the crowd. Tegan didn't need a crowd to witness his victory. He'd had a chip on his shoulder since the last time she'd bested him, and given Mira's weakened state, she was the prime target for his vengeance.

With a growl of fury, Mira summoned the energy to roll away from the foot Tegan swung at her. Dust blew up in the air, stinging her eyes as she maneuvered to avoid another kick.

"Not so tough now, are you?" the large male vampire taunted-ed.

Mira struggled to find her footing and keep away from his wild attacks. He was big and he was skilled, but he was also cocky. Many a formidable vampire had found their end through hubris, and Tegan was well on his way down that road. If Mira let him wear himself out, he'd eventually make a mistake, and that was when she needed to retaliate. Until that time, she'd have to duck and dodge as best she could, preserving what little energy she had for the right time to strike.

"Jealousy doesn't look good on you, Tegan," Mira taunted, hoping to rile him further.

"Shut up." Tegan swung wildly at her with one of his boulder-like fists.

Either her plan was working, or Tegan really was that bad a fighter. She smirked at the angry vampire. "Why don't you try to make me? Or are you afraid I'll muss up that pretty face of yours and your Patron won't want you anymore?"

It had never mattered much to her before; but now, weak as she was, Mira felt as if she were the only vampire alive who had not garnered a Patron. Servicing anyone wasn't something she particularly wanted to do, but in her current enfeebled state, she could certainly use the perks. Especially the additional rations. Slow healing and weakness could be avoided if Mira could just have a few sips of the fresh stuff. Nothing worked better than hot blood straight from a willing vein.

Tegan played right into her hands, taking the bait and charging her like a stampeding bull. Mira rolled away and hopped up to her feet just in time to avoid him. Tegan, however, overbalanced himself in an effort to stop when he missed his mark. He skidded to a halt, windmilling his arms to stop himself just before toppling over.

"It's not a fight if you run away." Tegan tried lamely to goad Mira. But her record spoke for itself. She was a killer. And if she hadn't been so weak, Tegan would have been under her boot already, begging for his life.

"Just giving you a sporting chance. I'd hate for you to limp away a complete failure." Mira kept her cocky tone, though the exertion was taking its toll. To the untrained eye she might have been doing well, but Mira was far from fighting form. Her muscles, weak and sore, responded more slowly than normal. Mira hoped to get the great big brute to wear himself out sooner rather than later, before he caught on to her weakness. Instead of overexerting himself, however, Tegan seemed to be enjoying this little to and fro. Feeding off it. He smiled as he attempted to strike again. She ducked away from his swing, but was barely quick enough. Mira felt the wind break across her face in the wake of Tegan's fist. She wasn't sure how much more she could take. Her body was nearly spent.

Tegan sneered and lunged again, putting all of his preternatural speed into the assault. Mira wasn't quick enough this time, and the force of his body colliding with hers knocked the wind from her lungs. She hit the dirt again, with Tegan's massive body crushing her under his bulk. Bones cracked. Pain shot through her chest. Mira was sure she'd just broken a rib or two, maybe more. That was going to take forever to heal without blood.

Tegan looked down at her and smiled. His eyes held that cocky glint that said he had other plans for her now that he had her pinned. And Mira would be damned if she'd allow him to follow through with them. She did the only thing she could. Baring her teeth, she threw her head forward and sank them into the bare skin of his chest.

It was only a moment. Only long enough to taste the coppery sweetness of his fresh blood, but that was more than she'd hoped for. By the time Tegan was able to throw her off, the revitalizing effects of his blood were already invigorating her, healing some of the damage he'd done to her body.

Involuntarily, Mira let out a moan of pure unadulterated pleasure. She couldn't help herself. Despite the source, hot blood fresh from the vein was a true delicacy. Her entire being awakened with new vigor. A wicked smile spread across Mira's lips. She slowly opened her eyes and locked onto Tegan's. While hers were full of wild energy, his showed pure rage, and that was the icing on the cake. She was ready for a real fight now.

"Now, let's continue."

Tegan knew before she had even risen to her feet that he'd lost. But being male and a warrior in his own right, he wouldn't let a little thing like an undefeated warrior fed on fresh blood stop him. Tegan stood and squared himself, ready to fight again, but Mira caught the quiver in his lips.

She stood and slowly cracked her neck and popped her back, making a little more of a show of it than she needed to. The pain of her broken ribs faded. They would be healed in moments as if they had never been damaged. All thanks to fresh blood.

Tegan watched every move Mira made, but made no move of his own to initiate the next fight.

"Scared now?" Mira said wickedly.

"Of you? Never." Tegan could lie all he wanted; the truth was in his eyes.

"Liar." Following Tegan's body posture and movement, Mira calculated the best time and angle to strike. Other than a slight twitch of his muscles, Tegan was not budging from his spot. Probably too scared. She'd just have to make the first move herself. Putting all of her renewed energy into action, she began with a roundhouse kick. Tegan easily side-stepped, caught Mira's foot, and spun her backwards. Small and lithe as she was, Mira was able to use the momentum to roll back up on to her feet and spin around to face her opponent as gracefully as if she were a dancer. As soon as she faced Tegan, she squared herself again, ready for the next attack.

"This ain't the ballet, sweetheart," Tegan spat at her, but there was more fear than anything else in his voice.

"Oh, but I do so love to dance." Mira dropped and swiped Tegan's legs. The larger vampire caught himself before he fell. Taking advantage of her opponent's momentary weakness, Mira delivered a few bone-crunching blows to Tegan's ribs.

Tegan dropped to the ground clutching his chest, but managed to roll away before Mira could deliver a nasty kick.

"This ain't dirt crawlers either, Tegan. Is this what you do in the arena? No wonder your record stinks."

That got Tegan fired up. He pushed himself back up to his feet and ran at Mira in a blind rage. She easily dodged his bullish attack and spun around to make sure he couldn't catch her from behind.

Tegan came at her again. She recognized the tactic: He was trying to overwhelm her, but he'd exhaust his reserves well before she would. Dodging him again, she threw a wild punch aimed at his gut. It caught him in the side with little effect.

"At least I fight fair," Tegan shouted. "No stolen blood."

"All's fair in love and war. Don't be a brat about it because you didn't think of it yourself."

The two squared off again. Sneering at each other. Mira studied his body movements, watching for any clue as to his next move. She wanted to end this... quickly.

The muscles in his leg twitched. He was going to lunge at her again, soon. She prepared herself.

He was quick, but she was quicker. Tegan came hard and fast, but Mira stepped out of the way and caught him by the arm. They twirled together for a moment before she used the momentum to throw him down to the ground. Tegan landed with a thud, his head slamming heavily against the hard-packed dirt.

Before she came down on him, she cocked her leg back and delivered a crushing kick to his ribs. The satisfying sound of bones breaking told her she had more than hit the mark, but it was Tegan's groan of pain that made her smile. That cocky bastard needed a good lesson in manners. She mounted him, setting herself hard on his chest, pressing down on those freshly broken ribs.

"We're done here." Mira placed a hand on either side of his head, ready to snap his neck if he tried anything stupid... hoping he would try something stupid, actually. Not that snapping his neck would kill the annoying vampire, but it would certainly bring her some instant gratification.

Overhead a voice spoke through speakers. "Training is over. Gladiators, resume your spots and wait for your handlers to retrieve you."

"You got lucky...this time," Mira snorted at him.

Tegan spat at Mira. "At least I didn't cheat."

As much as Mira wanted to rise to the occasion, his taunting wasn't worth it. The handlers were coming, and any additional aggression while they were around was bound to earn her more time in the lightbox. She needed her energy, what little of it she could spare, to formulate and execute her next escape attempt.

CHAPTER FIVE

Two **handlers came to retrieve Tegan**, but only one had shown to escort Mira. Luck must have been on her side. She smirked at Tegan as he was cuffed silently and nudged toward the exit. Clearly the loser, his shoulders slumped as he lumbered slowly behind one handler while the other followed, holding his UV torch at the ready. As much as she hated him, the sight of Tegan being taken away in such a manner tugged at her heartstrings. No matter what, arrogant prick that he was, he was still a vampire, one of *her* kind. Still a prisoner. And being treated this way was wrong.

When Tegan had finally disappeared, Mira looked around cautiously, secretly praying that her other handler would not show. Not that she was ever that lucky, but it would be nice.

"Where's your dance partner?" Mira knew she shouldn't have said it, but couldn't help herself. The fresh infusion of blood and a win in the training arena had her feeling quite cocky. And those handlers were big bullies as it was. Anything to get under their skin was a bonus for her.

"No funny business. Hold out your hands for cuffs," the handler snapped at her. She assumed it was her regular female handler, but the voice sounded strange. Mira had a sneaking suspicion that she had really shaken her previous handler up. That brought a new smile to her face.

This new handler was hiding her face behind a dark polycarbonate shield.

Humans really went to the extremes to prevent vampires from having any advantage. No eye contact – not that it would really matter if they did, the myth about vampires having mental capabilities and taking control of others thoughts was just that, a myth – but still, this human wasn't taking anything for granted. The oversized helmet with neck protection was, in Mira's opinion, a little overkill as well. Sure, she could go for the jugular, but unless she really intended to kill, there was no point. Blood loss was too quick at that artery. Of course, if she was intending to kill, flimsy plastic was not going to stop her. There were hundreds of ways to incapacitate a human without using her teeth. Problem was, as heavily guarded as the place was, it was generally not a smart idea to make trouble. Vampire strength or no, she was outnumbered. The only way out was through stealth, not bloodshed… no matter how tempting bloodshed was.

"Here!" Mira huffed and held out her arms, awaiting the cuffs.

A second handler appeared behind her and tossed the cuffs to the woman, who immediately clamped them around Mira's wrists. The initial sting of the silver made Mira groan. She hoped it hadn't been too loud. Showing weakness in front of the handlers was just inviting trouble, and she was already in enough trouble with them as it was.

"You're late," Mira said, hoping instead to cover the pain in her voice with taunting. "We were going to go to the party without you."

"Silence, slave." The pure hatred in the male handler's voice was unmistakable. His command was stern. She wished she could see his eyes. He could sound as mean as he wanted, but the truth, the fear, would show clearly in his eyes. Unfortunately, he too wore the dark shield hiding his features. "Let's get her back quickly," he said to his partner.

"Yeah. She's in a mood alright. And I don't feel like dealing with it," the female handler responded.

Mira felt the butt of a rifle jab into her back. "Move," the male handler ordered.

"Would it kill you to ask nicely?" Fresh blood and a win in the training arena had done wonders for her mood, but dealing with the handlers was quickly souring it.

"No talking," the male handler shouted.

"All right. All right. Sheesh. You people. So uptight."

"Shut up!" the male commanded again. He flashed his UV torch at the back of her neck.

Heat singed her skin. Ten times brighter than outdoor light, the UV torch's instant blast of pain took her breath away. Mira hadn't intended to, but as she flinched, shrinking back from the sting, she snapped her cuffs in two. She swung her free arm wide and hit the female handler so hard Mira knocked her to the ground.

The male had his torch at the ready, aimed right at Mira. "Don't move."

With the female handler down, and the hallway empty, it was now or never. She would have to be quick. Once an alarm was raised, it would be all over for her. But if she was fast enough, she might just make it to an exit. A full face blast from the UV torch was worth the risk. She lunged straight at the male handler, overtaking him. Itchy as his trigger finger was, he couldn't get a flash on her in time. She slammed him to the ground and then smashed his helmet a few times for good measure. He wouldn't be seriously hurt — those brain buckets were good for something — but when he did finally wake up, he'd have one hell of a headache. That was karma enough for her.

Secure in the knowledge that he was incapacitated and wouldn't be chasing her down anytime soon, Mira took off down the long dark corridor. Down one dark hallway and up another, Mira ran without knowing exactly where she was heading. Everything looked the same – no signs, no arrows to point in any specific direction. Every corridor had the identical stark walls, unmarked doors, and annoyingly bright fluorescent lights. Another way to deter escape. The entire place was set up like a giant maze. Was she heading toward the exit, or back around to where she had just come from? Still, hoping against all hope that she was heading in the right direction and not in circles, Mira continued on amid the blaring sirens and flashing red lights.

Round one turn and then another, Mira was beginning to feel hopelessly lost. She'd been escorted to the arena, training hall, and prison areas so many times she knew the routes by heart, but she was well out of bounds now.

Knowing she was short on time, Mira quickly rounded another corner and came face to face with a double set of guards.

Surprised and not as prepared as the handlers, they did not have their UV torches to hand. Mira had no problem incapacitating them and left them quietly on the ground, unconscious but still alive.

Before she had a chance to stand, the hair on the back of Mira's neck prickled. An uncomfortable weight of unseen eyes settled on her. Dread sank to the pit of her stomach. Busted...and so close to escaping. Someone else was there, watching her. She felt it, but what was more unsettling was the fact they had yet to announce themselves. Guards would shoot first and ask questions later. Someone lurking in the shadows... there was no telling what game they'd be playing.

Mira turned around and stood next to the guard she had just felled. It didn't take much for her to find the source of her unease. A pair of mossy green eyes scrutinized her from the opposite end of the hall.

Heart pounding, she stared back at the man attached to those quizzical eyes. Human, no doubt. But he didn't carry a weapon. Nor was there any fear in those green eyes of his. On the contrary, alone in a dark corridor, he stood his ground, lifting his head, and stared Mira down like an alpha from some long lost wolf pack.

The strangeness of his manner caught Mira by surprise. For a few moments too long, she stood dumbfounded, trying to process who he was and what her next move should be. His face seemed oddly familiar, though at the moment she couldn't place where she'd seen him before.

The strange man was tall and well built, but that really didn't matter much. Mira could take down vampires larger than she with no problem. But that wasn't the thing stopping her from making a move. Judging by the deep plum of his suit, he was a man of some power. Only the Elite – those in the ruling class – were ever permitted to wear such an audacious color. As desperate as Mira was at that moment, she needed to tread carefully. Being caught escaping — again — would earn her more time in the lightbox, but injuring an Elite could have her staked out in the middle of town square awaiting the dawn.

"Aren't you going to finish him?" the man asked, his tone calm, soothing, as if he genuinely wanted to know the answer.

"Why don't I finish you instead?" She hoped the warning in her voice would be enough to deter him, but still the man remained unfazed, like some stoic statue across the hallway. What was he playing at? And why was he just standing there, calmly, giving her every opportunity to strike? Did he really place so little value on his life?

"You could kill me, sure, but ask yourself how that is going to help your situation." Spoken like a true Elite. He had to be up to something.

She didn't like the smugness in tone, but felt at a loss as to how to continue. She could be on him in a fraction of a second. Crush his windpipe, and maybe buy herself a few more minutes to find the exit, but she was lost and had already wasted too much time. However, her inaction was almost certain to earn her some additional reprisal as well.

The corner of his lip quirked up. "I take it by your lack of response, that you've decided against harming me?"

Damn him! He knew she couldn't take the risk. "For the moment, I guess." Mira did not let her own uncertainty leach out into her voice. She attempted to sound self-assured, as if she were the one in charge at that moment.

"Well." He let out a little sigh. "I'm pleased to hear that." The strange man smiled congenially. "But, we will have to sort out what to do with you. It appears you're out of bounds here."

"You gonna help me back to my cell?" She threw her contempt at him. *Bastard Elite!* What did he know about boundaries?

"The thought had crossed my mind, yes."

"Of course it had. Too bad I was heading in the other direction." Mira casually flicked her hand toward the hallway to her left.

"Wonderful, seeing as that is the way back to the cell block."

He was toying with her, like a cat with a mouse, Mira was sure of it. Whatever he had planned was sure to end with her enduring more punishment time in the lightbox. Mira pursed her lips. She wanted more than anything to be rid of him, but at this point she'd dug herself in too deeply to back out. Punishment or no, she had to play his little game. The alternative — certain death — was not worth the risk.

"Relax. I was only joking with you." He held out his hands in mock surrender. "Please. I mean you no harm. But, in all seriousness, you know you can't leave. Not like this."

The way he delivered those last words piqued her interest. "Are you saying there is a better way to leave?"

Mira picked up the heavy footfall of a few more guards headed in her direction. The human must have heard them too, because for a brief moment he turned his attention to the hallway.

"Perhaps. But that all starts with how you manage the next few moments." The Elite closed the distance between them, stepping confidently toward her as if she were as harmless as a kitten.

Part of her wanted to kill him and move on, even if there was no chance of escape, but the truth was plain: Her hesitation had ruined all chances she might have had of getting away.

Mira's shoulders slumped. "Fine. What help can you be?"

His moss-green eyes met hers and for a moment Mira felt they were on even footing. "Let me take you back, myself. No weapons." There was a genuine kindness in the way he spoke that did not fit his species or station. He held up his hands as proof that he had nothing to harm her with. "Just walk calmly with me, and I will ensure no reprisal comes to you."

Utterly confused, Mira could no longer hold the anger in her voice. "Why would you do this for me?"

'Politician' was her first thought. How much publicity would he receive for single-handedly bringing in a vampire?

"Why didn't you kill those guards?" he responded with equal measure of curiosity.

She glanced down at the unconscious men and felt a twinge of sorrow. Their breathing was shallow but steady. They'd be out for at least a little longer, but when they woke, with heads pounding, they'd wish they were dead. "They got what was coming to them, but just because they're pricks doesn't mean they deserve death. They're just trained idiots doing their job."

One of the Elite's eyebrows quirked up. "Interesting," he chuckled. "They aren't always the smartest of the litter. But don't you need their blood? Don't you crave every last drop?"

"Of course I crave blood, like you do a hamburger or potato chips, but, like you, I do not need to gorge myself on them all day long. Only a little at a time is needed to satiate my hunger. Any more than that is gluttony." Mira hoped he caught her little jab at him. Those of the Elite were no strangers to indulging in whatever they wanted, whenever they wanted it. They were the definition of gluttons. "The pint or two I need daily will not kill anyone."

Embarrassment flashed across the Elite's face for the briefest of moments before it vanished. "I guess I always assumed…. Never mind. Come. I hear the guards approaching. Allow me to escort you back, and we'll chat about all of this later."

He stepped forward cautiously and lifted his hand to grasp her by the arm.

Reflexively, Mira's lip curled into a sneer. She didn't want to trust this man — humans could never be trusted — but she had no other choice.

Allowing him to take hold of her arm, she gave the Elite a look of warning and a quick flash of her fangs.

Looking as if he was trying to remain unfazed by her feral growl, he held his head high and pierced her with his mossy green gaze. "Follow my lead."

"Fine," she managed to say, though she had many other choice words in mind.

A group of five handlers came to a sudden halt in front of the Elite. Masks covered their faces, so Mira couldn't see the expressions, but the surprise and shock was clear in their gasps.

"Regent," the lead guard called out, bowing his head immediately. "Are you okay?"

Regent? That's where she'd seen him before. From her vantage point down in the arena, she'd never gotten a good look at his face, but she remembered seeing the man eating his steak at the last battle. He was as Elite as you could get in the Iron Gate. Second only to the Magistrate who ruled over all the human cities, he was top dog. Why the hell was he helping her? Now Mira's curiosity was really piqued.

"Thank you for the quick response, Handlers. But the situation is under control. I'm just having a little chat here with, I'm sorry, what was your name?"

No human ever asked her that before. Her handlers called her by her cell number; her master called her slave. The rest of the world called her gladiator. Why was this human, this Elite, pretending to be so nice to her? "Uh… Mira."

One of the Handlers grasped his UV torch and took a step toward the pair.

The Regent smiled congenially. "Thank you, Mira. Yes, I was having a little chat with her about conditions in the lower cell block." He tightened his grasp on her arm as he addressed the armed Handlers. The warmth of his large hand felt deliciously wrong on her cold skin.

"Sir, please step away from the vampire." The lead handler held his UV torch up at the ready. Behind him the other handlers had their weapons raised as well.

"Ease up, gentlemen. We're fine. But, if you'll escort us, I need to return Mira to her place now."

No one would dare to disobey an Elite. Grumbling behind their masks, they trained their UV torches on Mira, no doubt longing for the opportunity to blast her with them. The lead Handler looked down to his wrist and punched in a code on a thick electronic bracer, his com-link. "Central. We've found the missing gladiator. Returning her to the lower cell block now."

A few moments of static followed by another voice confirming what had been said. A second later the alarms silenced. Mira was never more thankful. Their shrill screams were extra annoying to her enhanced hearing.

The head guard waved them forward. "This way, sir." He led them down the corridor to the left.

The Regent, still grasping Mira's arm firmly, set the slow pace as they walked back to her cell.

All eyes were on them — human security and vampire alike — as they walked quietly through the cell block. Some vampires stood from their mattresses and gasped as Mira passed their cells, being handled by the Regent himself.

"Code, please," the Regent demanded as they reached Mira's cell.

The guard lifted his wrist and punched a few buttons on his com-link bracer, and then entered the ten digit code into the lock panel.

Mira noticed immediately that the tones had changed. She did not have to look down to know that the code was different. *Damn, they were quick!* The cell doors opened and the Regent released Mira. For the first time in years, rather than being tossed, shoved, or thrown down, Mira casually walked into her own cell. The experience was quite novel.

"We will talk again very soon. Do you have a Patron?" The Elite's congenial tone continued to shock her, even more than the fact that he'd asked her Patron status. Again his curious moss-green eyes met hers without animosity. This man was a complete conundrum to her. And he wanted to see her again? Possibly be her Patron?

Taken aback, Mira stuttered, trying to find the words. "N...sorry... no, I don't."

"I will speak with your Owner." With that, the Elite turned and walked away.

The cell doors closed, but Mira remained standing where she was, dumbfounded.

CHAPTER SIX

Time moved slowly for Mira. Running the events of the evening through her mind, she stared up at the ceiling as if it might somehow hold some answers for her. She should be dead. Or at the very least strung up in the Hall of Punishment awaiting her next torture. Instead, she had been allowed to return to her cell, unharmed and unpunished, with a potential offer of patronage. There had to be something else going on.

Soft bells chimed seven times, marking the hour. Morning. Not that it made any difference to Mira. Even if she could stand the sunlight, she was still a creature of the night. She should be sleeping. She needed sleep. There was no telling what the day would bring, and it was in her best interest to be rested and ready for action.

Mira tried to convince herself to relax. Tried to order her mind to clear. It almost worked, until she heard the creak of metal doors opening. Someone was coming, and not just any someone. Mira expected the worst when she heard her Owner's fast paced clip-clop echoing down the corridor. She'd rather deal with her handlers or go another round in the training arena with Tegan before dealing with Olivia.

"What the hell did you do this time?" Angry and demanding, Olivia's shrill call pierced the early morning silence.

Mira had too many questions running through her head at that point and no answers, or at least no good answer for herself or Olivia. She knew no matter what she said, it was bound to aggravate her already annoyed Owner anyway.

Before Mira could form a coherent sentence for her Owner, Olivia barked, "Talk. Now. I want to know everything that happened." Her foot tapped out an impatient rhythm on the concrete floor.

Mira didn't have to look up to know her Owner would be staring her down, hands on her hips, positively seething with anger. Not because she was upset that Mira had not answered her yet. That was simply Olivia's normal stance when dealing with Mira. Rather than stand on ceremony, she continued to lie on her mattress. "I tried to escape. I got caught. I'm awaiting punishment."

"Oh, and I wish I could give it. Trust me, you troublesome little leech. Do you know how much that escape attempt of yours cost me?"

Olivia's tone was dangerous, but Mira just couldn't help herself, now that she knew she was in the clear.

"You're good for it," Mira said, not bothering to hide her smile.

"Oh, I can afford it, but you'll be the one paying back the damages." Olivia's angry voice had suddenly turned wicked. She laughed, and that piqued Mira's interest.

She sat up and looked at her Owner. "The usual pound of flesh I assume? Can we postpone the tanning salon until after my nap? I'm a bit tired at the moment." She knew she shouldn't have said it, but she just couldn't help herself. She loved getting a rise out of her Owner – or any human, for that matter.

"You think you're untouchable, don't you? That's all about to change. You'll learn a new meaning of the word 'touched' soon enough. Well, after you're prepped, of course."

Prepped?

Olivia sounded as if she were truly enjoying this new devious plan of torture. Mira chanced a glance up to her Owner's face. A smile, twisted and cruel, met her, and the glint in Olivia's hazel eyes said that Mira was in for a whole new world of trouble she'd yet to encounter.

"You got yourself a Patron, dearie."

Olivia must have mistaken her gasp as a sign of fright because she cackled loud enough to wake George in the cell next to her.

He really followed through? Fear was the farthest thing from her mind. She'd service anyone she had to in order to get a little comfort at this point. No, shock had stolen her ability to express anything at that moment. Mira couldn't believe the Elite had actually followed through. There had to be something she was missing, some angle, some reason. Humans never did anything nice… not without an ulterior motive.

"And a rich one at that. So, you had better be on your best behavior and do whatever he wants. And I do mean anything that he wants, whatever, wherever, and however. Do you hear me?"

Mira heard her all right, and more than that, she heard the dollar signs in her Owner's voice. "He's called for you to meet him later tonight, so I need to have you prepped and ready." That brought another wicked smile to her Owner's face.

Mira wasn't sure what being prepped entailed, but it couldn't be any worse than the lightbox. "Bring on your worst."

"I was hoping you'd say that."

CHAPTER SEVEN

Escorted by her two handlers, with Olivia leading the way, Mira was ushered to a place referred to affectionately by George as the 'spa.'

The inside of the spa was a place Mira had never before earned the privilege of seeing. She'd expected it to look lavish. George had made it sound positively magical, but other than the strange stations with equipment she couldn't imagine the uses for, the place was just as dreary as the rest of the prison. Flat gray walls, black and white tile floors, and thick steel doors at the entrance and exit. Curiously, there was one door — more like a window — in the back corner of the room that was not steel like the rest. It was made of a thick pane of glass and led into a small room completely covered in tile, just big enough for a single person to stand in.

She'd never seen such an odd space.

The butt of a UV torch hit her in the back. "Move," the handler ordered.

A woman dressed in a skin-tight black full body suit sauntered up to Olivia. She looked down at her clipboard and ran a long red manicured fingernail down the page. "You're the works, right?"

Olivia smirked at Mira before answering. "I want her showered, plucked, shaved, trimmed, and for the love of god, do something with those nails. She has a wealthy Patron to impress."

"You heard the client. Get this leech ready to be presented to her Patron." She snapped her fingers, and two other humans, females in matching black body suits, appeared seemingly out of thin air and rushed forward.

A shiver of fear raced down Mira's spine. Torture she could endure, even if that meant more time in the lightbox, but this "works" treatment her Owner had ordered — waxing, plucking, nails, and whatever else it entailed — scared the hell out of her.

Without another word, her dirty tunic was ripped from her body and tossed aside like the garbage it was.

Mira had to fight the instinct to lash out at the trio of women stripping her down and scrutinizing her naked body. She'd love to wipe their smug expressions right off their pretty little faces. Perhaps rip out their tightly braided ponytails and strangle them; but she knew she'd never get away with it. She'd just have to ignore their taunts and whispered comments about her filthy condition.

Once the trio was done inspecting her, they ushered her toward the strange tile room. "We'll have her washed and ready by seven this evening," Mira heard one say as the glass door opened and she was pushed inside.

A low clicking sound ran up the walls seconds before the jets began. Hot water and steam assaulted her from every angle. The initial shock and hot sting subsided and Mira relaxed, letting the water wash away the grime. Showers were a luxury only afforded to vampires with additional funding, something she'd never earned. Until now, bathing for her had consisted of a lukewarm bucket of water and a rag.

Another set of clicks ran up the wall behind the tiles and the spray turned soapy. It foamed on her skin, carrying a subtle hint of orange blossom and citrus, a smell that reminded her of the orange groves that had grown near her home as a human. The foam seemed to expand on her skin, growing as it if it were feeding on the dirt clinging to her body. The sensation was shocking and intriguing at the same time. She could see why George enjoyed coming to this place. They might have been rude, but this shower alone made up for it. Never before had she felt so pampered.

Another click, and the deliciously hot water returned and melted away the foamy bubbles encasing her body. The water not only took with it the dirt and grime, but melted away some of the stress and tension in her body. Try as she might, it was hard to remain alert and on edge while the heat and pressure of the water worked its magic on her muscles.

When the shower finished, hot air filled the chamber, blowing like a cyclone in the small room. Shocking and sudden, it startled Mira, but just like with the water, the heat of the wind had a soothing effect that made it hard for her to remain on edge. She took a breath and let the warm air do its thing and dry the beads of water from her body.

Just when she thought she was finished in the shower, one final jet gently spritzed some kind of citrus-scented oil on her.

The clicks behind the tile stopped, and the glass door opened by itself. Mira turned and stepped out of the box, making no attempt to cover herself, and awaited her next instruction.

A wicked smile played in her Owner's sharp features. "Well, now, at least you don't stink. But you're far from ready to present to your Patron." She turned to the trio of women. "I'll be back at seven to retrieve her." Not waiting for confirmation, she and the two handlers walked out through the steel doors.

The shower had been quite refreshing, Mira thought. She hoped the rest of these treatments would be just as pleasant. George had spoken highly of this place. Perhaps it was not as bad as she feared.

"What's next?" Mira asked.

One of the trio of women held up a jar of melted wax. "Hair removal."

The unusually eager way she said it stole away Mira's feelings of relaxation and contentment. This, she knew, would not be as nice as the shower had been.

Hours later, plucked, tweezed, waxed, and threaded, Mira had endured the removal of every hair on her body. What hair remained, on top of her head, had been washed, cut, and styled so that her short hair framed around her face. Rather than the tunic and linen pants she was accustomed to wearing, Mira had been given a proper dress. Knee-length, the black and pink sheath dress felt unbelievably soft. Nothing like what she was used to wearing. They'd even given her shoes to wear. Those, however, were not as comfortable as her sandals had been. Tight and toe-pinching, these shoes had heels that made her feel as if she was walking on stilts. If you could call what she was doing 'walking' – more like trying hard not to fall with each wobbly step she took.

By the time Olivia returned to retrieve her, Mira was almost unrecognizable.

"That'll do," Olivia said, with no hint as to whether or not she actually approved. "Let's get you moving."

CHAPTER EIGHT

U p an unfamiliar flight of stairs, Mira, her Owner, and the two handlers exited into a brightly lit lobby. Unlike other places Mira had been before, this place radiated an almost cheerful nature. Warm and inviting compared to the drab gray of the prisons, Mira felt as if she had entered a whole new world. Colors she'd forgotten existed were splashed all over paintings adorning the russet-colored walls. Crisp white trim framed the doorways. Comfortable-looking wingback chairs flanked a set of elevator doors that had been polished to a mirror-like finish.

As if to remind Mira of her place, one of the handlers nudged her a little too harshly with the butt of his UV torch. "Quit gawking. Move."

Olivia took the lead, heading straight to the polished steel elevator doors. She pressed the button, which illuminated to a bright orangey-red. "Your Patron keeps you in luxury. Remember this. If you so much as annoy him in any way, I'll send you to the lightbox for a week."

"Got it," Mira said, with as much enthusiasm as she could muster. She knew what she had to do and didn't need the reminder. She would do whatever was needed to keep herself alive and hopefully give herself another chance to make an escape. Even as they entered the elevator and exited on the top floor, Mira was paying close attention to every detail, looking for ways out, making sure she remembered exactly how they got to and from all of the new places she'd seen this day.

The hallway they entered was just as warm and inviting as the lobby they'd left. At the end of the hall sat a large mirror. Mira had not yet seen herself after she'd been cleaned. In truth, it had been years since Mira had seen a real reflection. She'd seen images of herself on the big screen in the arena, covered in blood and gore, but nothing like this, a close up, clear look at herself. She hardly recognized the woman staring back at her. Her face, her eyes, her hair — everything was so alien. What was most disturbing though was that in this light, she almost looked human. All the makeup they'd slathered on her covered up the pale skin and the bruised-looking bags under her eyes. Even her hair seemed to have an unnatural glow to its raven color. She supposed that was to make her more presentable to humans, but it made her feel a little like a clown.

The handlers escorted her to the doorway of her Patron's suite.

Olivia gave Mira a quick once over, nodding approvingly, before pressing the doorbell.

When the doors parted, Mira met the muted green eyes of the man who'd thwarted her escape attempt the previous day. The Regent. The most powerful man in the city. And her new Patron. The irony of it almost made her laugh.

"Leave her with me." His voice was confident, his smile seductive. The little quirk up at the corner of his lips gave his entire face an impish quality. He might be an attractive man, if Mira were attracted to humans. But that was a moot point. He was her Patron, and she'd have to do whatever it was he wanted of her, attraction or no.

"She's a skilled warrior, sir," one of the handlers replied. "Quite dangerous."

"She knows what's good for her. This little treat will not harm me," her Patron replied.

Mira sneered at the way he called her a treat. Like she was some little plaything, no more real than a doll. Of course, that was probably closer to the truth now than anything else, dressed up as she was. She'd been giftwrapped for him like some present for New Year Jubilee.

"I'll leave my guards at your door. Call if you need anything," Olivia replied and bowed low, respectfully, to her Regent.

"You'll hear from me when I need you." He reached out, grasping Mira by the arm in the same way he'd done the previous day, and pulled her into his room.

The automatic door shut behind her with a soft click.

The Regent released her and walked further into the suite. "Come. Mira, right?"

He damn well knew her name, why was he playing?

"Sit, relax. Please." He indicated to a plush couch in the center of the room. "Would you care for refreshment?"

"What is your game?" Mira had no patience for pleasantries.

"I thought we could continue our chat from yesterday, with a little more privacy." The Regent unbuttoned the jacket of his purple suit and laid it carefully on the arm of the couch.

The thought of what was sure to come curled Mira's lips. She tried to hide it, remembering what her Owner had warned, but couldn't quite cloak the contempt in her voice. "Why? What do you want from me? Why are you playing nice?"

"Easy now, Mira." He held his hands out as if to emphasize the calm in his voice. "I want nothing from you but a chat. You're a curiosity. I want to know more about you."

"Why, so you can exploit me and my kind later?"

"So I can understand." Impatience began to overtake his congenial tone.

"Understand what?"

"To get right to the point, then: I want to know how a blood savage can show so much humanity."

"Humanity?" Mira laughed at the word. "Humans are the savages. Look at how you treat my kind."

"Kill or be killed, Mira. Survival..."

Forgetting for a moment that she was supposed to keep her Patron happy, Mira yelled, "Don't feed me that bullshit." Almost shaking with rage, she stopped herself from advancing on him and doing something she might regret. "My kind are no more murderous than yours, and yet we're the ones behind bars, tortured, forced to perform like dancing monkeys. Forced to kill our own kind… at your command!"

Seemingly unfazed by her emotional outburst, he responded, "You drink blood…"

"Yes. Because that's the only thing we can stomach. What's your excuse for spilling so much?"

"We're getting off on the wrong foot here. Let's calm down." He set himself down smoothly onto the end of the couch. "This is exactly why I wanted you here. I feel as if I may be misinformed about many things, especially your… species. I would like the opportunity to know more. To understand. Please…" He patted the spot next to him. "Enlighten me."

Wary of what his true motives were, Mira had no choice but to indulge his questions. She had to play the game, as George had so often told her. Walking to the couch to take her seat, Mira glanced around, noting all of the windows and doors in the room. What few there were. The suite itself, though opulent, was cozy. The sitting room appeared to make up the bulk of it. A small door off to her left must have been the bedroom area, as she saw no other door except for the one through which she'd entered.

A smallish curtained window sat above a computer-generated fireplace. Hardly big enough to afford a decent view, it didn't appear to open, either. Certainly not big enough to use for any type of escape. Even if it had been, they were ten floors up. A jump from that height would most certainly result in broken bones, and she wasn't so sure she'd be able to heal fast enough to make a break for it. The place was probably swarming with guards and handlers too. Hope of escape from this room was slim to none.

"Fine. What do I call you? Patron, Regent, Grand High Poobah, what?" She set herself heavily down on the couch and almost sprang back up from the bounciness of the cushion.

"Where are my manners? Lucian Stavros." He stood and bowed. Mira found such a show of respect odd. She still questioned his motives, but at least he was playing his part well enough to be almost believable.

"Do you need anything for refreshment?" His voice was hesitant.

"You already know the answer to that. No. I'm fine."

"The suite is fully stocked for all needs." His confidence wavered enough for Mira to catch the worried look in his green eyes. I am quite sure there is a supply of... blood for you here."

"No. I'm fine. Let's just get this over with."

Lucian took his seat and smoothed out his purple suit pants. He took a deep, almost calming breath before speaking. "I do not wish to use you, Mira. I know you don't believe me. Can we please just talk?"

Whether he admitted it or not, he was using her. Information, sex, whatever his pleasure, his only reason for having her here was to serve his needs. No matter how politely he was doing it. Mira was not about to forget that. She'd give him only what she had to and nothing more.

"Whatever you need of me, sir." Mira's reply was cold, emotionless.

He smiled politely. "Well, let's start simply with your history. Tell me. How long have you been in the system?"

"Longer than I care to remember."

"And have you been a gladiator the entire time?"

"Yes."

"Do you enjoy it?"

"No." What kind of a question was that? How could she take any pleasure from having to fight and kill her kind? Humans were either truly savage or clueless.

"Of course not. How rude of me to ask. Were you ever offered any other jobs?"

"I was not suited to anything else."

"Why not? You're a vampire, certainly strong enough to work other jobs."

"My attitude says otherwise."

"I'm beginning to understand that."

"What is that supposed to mean?"

"Well, you're not being very cooperative or pleasant."

"Why should I be? I'm a slave. I'm being used every day to serve the desires of humans. Even now, you're only interested in what information I can provide. Call it what you will. Put your positive spin on it, but all you're doing is using me to indulge your morbid curiosity. Don't expect me to be all cheerful about it."

"I may be curious, yes, but have you considered that the information you provide might actually help you? I'm in a position to not only make your life better, but also the lives of your kind too. I am the Regent."

She hated that he had a very good point, but also doubted he would actually do anything to aid in the better treatment of her kind. Mira reminded herself again that he was her Patron. She really shouldn't piss him off. "Apologies, Regent. Please ask your questions."

He didn't look convinced by her change of tone, but continued. "Okay. What did you do before you... ah... came to us?"

Like she was going to tell him that. Now she understood his true motivation. He wanted, like others before him, to know about the safe haven.

"I lived."

"And how long have you been a vampire?"

"Longer than I can remember."

He sighed in frustration and stood. "This works better when you actually participate in the conversation."

"See, that's the problem. Other than to save my own skin by not pissing you off too much, Patron, I don't have a reason to do that."

"You don't trust me?"

"Why should I? You're human."

"I'm trying... That's why I offered to be your Patron. It is a show of good faith to you that I intend to keep my word. You are safe here with me, under my care."

"You live in this opulence, while I sleep on a cold hard mattress with barely a scrap of cloth to cover me. You eat steaks and watch my kind kill each other for sport, while I spend my days fighting for survival. You order the death of my kind on a whim and allow all manner of atrocities to be done to us. You cannot ask me to trust you simply because you paid for me to have a shower and some clean clothes to wear."

"I see. I think we are done for now." He looked down to the com-link around his wrist and pressed a button. "You may return her now."

He looked back to Mira. "It's a two-way street, Mira. At least I am making some effort. Think on that when you return to your cell."

The door behind them opened and the two handlers stepped through. They scowled at Mira and one of them grunted, "Get up."

She stood without a second look back at Lucian and walked to the door.

CHAPTER NINE

T he cell door shut behind her. She was back home in the tiny prison smelling of dirt and mold, filled with the agonizing cries of tortured souls. Coming from the opulent suite she'd just been escorted out of, it was a harsh reminder of who she was and how tiny and insignificant in the grand scheme of things.

Mira wiped the lipstick from her mouth and collapsed onto her mattress. She knew she shouldn't have pissed Lucian off. Why couldn't she have hidden her hatred of him and his kind? Was her pride really worth this? She could have just given him some of the information he wanted to keep him happy. Would it really have been so bad to play along? She could have glossed over the important stuff. Told him whatever bullshit he wanted to hear, and enjoyed a few moments of luxury. She could have benefited from extra blood; healed, built up strength, renewed energy to escape. No. She just had to let her anger and her ego get the better of her. Screw everything up.

"You okay, girl?" George asked. He appeared at the bars with a hopeful smile. "You weren't gone very long."

"I don't want to talk about it." Mira rolled away from her friend. Even if she had wanted to talk to someone, how could she possibly explain how horribly she'd failed?

"The first time is always the worst. It gets easier. He didn't try to hurt you, did he?"

As if he could actually hurt her. Mira was a champion gladiator. No. The only thing that was about to hurt her was herself.

She'd probably lost her first and only Patron ever. "Go away, George. I said I don't want to talk about it."

"You don't always have to be the tough girl. None of us like this sort of thing, but we do it to save our skin."

"I will find a way out of here." She said it more to herself than to George.

"Yeah. I'm sure you will. But for now, try and make the best of it. Whenever my Patron calls, I try to imagine I'm laying with a hot Island girl. Caramel skin, long dark hair, mmmmmm. You might try it. Next time he calls, just imagine me."

Despite her self-loathing, Mira let out a small chuckle. "Thanks, I'll do that."

"If it's any consolation. I heard you're not going back into the arena this weekend."

"What?" Mira shot up from the mattress. "Why not?"

"Don't sound all eager to get into a fight now."

"I'm not, it's just... I've never had a weekend without a fight."

"A Patron is good for some things."

Had Lucian really stopped her from fighting? Was it something she'd said? He may have called her a curiosity, but she was the one completely perplexed by him. Why, of all people, would an Elite attempt to keep her safe? It just didn't make any sense.

CHAPTER TEN

Mira stood outside of her Patron's door awaiting his answer. He'd called her up in the middle of the day. She'd barely had time to comprehend what was happening before she was yanked out of her cell and thrown into the hot steam shower. As much as she enjoyed that new luxury, she'd have liked it to be after she'd had a chance to fully wake up.

"Stand clear," the handler shouted at her, and roughly gripped her shoulder in an attempt to pull her backwards. The lock clicked softly and Lucian's door slid open.

Her Patron stood on the other side, plum collared shirt unbuttoned down the front and black silk trousers belted at the waist. Despite her aversion to humans for the way they treated her kind, Mira couldn't help but appreciate the bit of washboard stomach she could see. Lucian might have been Elite, but he was no fatted pig like so many others.

"Good day, Mira," he addressed her directly.

She nodded but said nothing.

Lucian turned to the handlers. "I'll take it from here."

With a grunt of agreement, the handler relaxed his grip. Mira shrugged away from him and stepped inside her Patron's suite.

Before the door had a chance to fully close behind her, Mira blurted out, "Did you have me pulled from this weekend's match?"

Shock at her outrage had clearly stolen Lucian's voice. Mira watched the confusion play across his furrowed brow.

"Yes, I did. Why?"

Mira took a breath, trying to calm the anger in her voice. She had already started off on the wrong foot with him. She was lucky he still wanted to be her Patron. "Why are you interfering with my life?"

"Sorry, I thought you abhorred killing. I was trying to do you a favor."

"You want to do me favors, get me the hell out of this place."

"Watch your tone, please."

"Why? Or you'll have the handlers put me in the lightbox?"

"No. But the walls are not thick enough to conceal raised voices. Do you really want to alert the handlers to our conversations?"

He was right and Mira knew it. She let out a deep sigh. "Sorry."

"And what is a lightbox, anyway?"

"Torture." She blurted the word out. There was no way he could be that clueless, could he?

"I'm not aware of any torture. I understand there are... reprisals for infractions committed by the... vampires kept below."

If she hadn't been so enraged by his response she might have laughed at the business-like way he said it. "And what exactly do you think these 'reprisals' are?"

He stood silently for a moment, his brow creasing and relaxing. Mira could almost see the wheels turning inside his head. He really didn't know what was going on.

"Reduced rations, I assume. Perhaps lack of social time." Lucian was grasping at some kind of intelligent answer, but Mira knew better.

It was all she could do not to burst out into maniacal laughing. "What the hell is social time? Do you mean training? Otherwise known as the mini-arena? Do you know how many of my kind die during these... reprisals?"

His cheeks flushed a delicious shade of crimson. It was hard for Mira not to stare, nor to begin to salivate at the sudden jump of his heart rhythm.

"I was unaware." Lucian tried to compose himself, but his heart betrayed his embarrassment.

"Yeah, it sounds like there is a lot you're unaware of. And you're a Regent?"

"I'll thank you not to poke fun. My station demands a little respect." There it was, the authority. There was no mistaking that arrogance and self-important tone.

Mira stood stiffly at attention and wiped all emotion from her face. "Yes, sir."

His composure wavered. Lucian threw his hands in the air and almost growled in frustration. "You know, I have done nothing but try and be helpful, and you throw nothing but scorn and mockery at me."

"Permission to speak freely, Regent?"

"You see? This behavior. If I were any other man, you'd have lost yourself a Patron. But I am not just any other man, and I am trying to show you exactly that. Despite your numerous attempts at trying my patience. Yes, Mira. Speak freely, dammit!"

She'd overstepped and she knew it, but the damage had already been done. Mira softened her tone a bit. "Perhaps instead of trying to help me in ways you feel are best, maybe you should try asking what is needed."

"I did try asking, last time you were here. But, as I recall, someone was very uncooperative."

"Can't be helped. You can't be trusted."

"And we're back to this again. What if I told you I was working on a way to get you out of here?"

Mira's eyebrow quirked up, but she tried to hold the rest of her face still. "Why?"

Why indeed? Was he hoping to catch her off guard? Let her run and take him straight to where the vampire safe haven was? Yes. That had to be his plan.

"Tell me about life in the arena." He walked to the couch and sat. Without looking back at her, he picked up a glass from the side table next to him, took a sip, and then set it down. He seemed to be moving slowly, purposefully, as if to ensure there was enough time to let the weight of his words sink in. "Let's forget our mistrust for now and just enlighten me on what it's like to live your life here."

She did not move from her spot. She didn't want to give him the satisfaction of making her come over to him and spill her secrets. Mira couldn't figure him out. If he was truly clueless and willing to help, she couldn't be sure, but she saw no harm in telling him what went on in the arena and the pits — and especially in training — leaving no gory detail undescribed. She made sure to spend extra time on the lightbox, the starvation, the painful punishments–like having their fingernails and toenails removed when they had lost fights but had not been condemned to death. When she was through and satisfied she had shocked and horrified Lucian enough, she smiled and innocently said, "Have you heard enough?"

Lucian turned from his spot on the couch, his hand covering the horror of his expression. "Mira, I didn't know."

"What did you know?" Mira scoffed. "Or did you even care?"

Lucian stood and came to Mira, taking her hands in his, a small gesture, but one that added an infinite amount of confusion to Mira's anger.

"I know it is not an excuse," Lucian said with sincerity, "but I grew up with this – the arena, the games – as entertainment. I never actually gave thought to what happened behind the scenes."

Mira threw down his hands and took a step back from Lucian. "But you were okay with us killing each other in the public eye?"

"Again… not an excuse. But I was raised to believe you were all savage creatures. It's not the same."

"Bullshit!"

To Mira's surprise, he let her foul language slide. If she'd said that to anyone else, Mira would have surely gotten a blast from a UV torch, or a slap across the mouth at the very least. Even more surprising, Lucian appeared to nod agreeably. "I know. And I'm not defending myself or the people who raised and educated me."

"So what changed your mind?"

"I'm not entirely sure my mind is changed, but you…"

"What about me?"

"You're… not… what I expected."

Mira wasn't quite sure how to respond to that.

"You could have easily killed those guards. You could have killed me."

"Yes, I could. And I'm still considering it."

Lucian sucked in a breath, but his expression remained calm, flat, as if her words had not shaken him.

"But I don't kill unless I have to." And she wouldn't have wished that death sentence on herself. Getting caught killing a human of any class was a one-way ticket to a flaming death. Not that Lucian wouldn't already know that, but at this point, her motives would still appear pure.

"I see that. And hope you'll not have to anytime soon." He smiled congenially, but Mira could see the discomfort behind his eyes. "That is why I had you removed from fighting duties."

"You can't keep me from the arena."

"You really want to go back there?"

"People will ask questions if I don't fight. I've got a reputation. And so do you! What do you think people will say when the Regent's favorite suddenly stops fighting in the arena?"

The corner of his lip quirked up. "Smart and politically minded. You are so full of surprises."

"As are you." She still couldn't figure him out. Part of her, a very small part, wanted to trust him; he seemed so sincere. But he was a Regent, an Elite. A human. They could never be trusted. He had to have some ulterior motive.

"Fine. I will not interfere with your arena schedule, but if we are to help one another, I'll need you to be a good girl and play nice."

The way he said "good girl" had her hackles up, but she tried to tell herself it was meant in a playful way. "What is it exactly that you want from me?" She hoped for a straight answer, but doubted seriously she'd get one.

"My interest in you is genuine. You perplex me. I want to know the truth about your kind. For my own personal understanding. Nothing more. Nothing less."

The com-link bracer round Lucian's wrist buzzed, and a mechanically enhanced male voice said, "Regent, sorry to bother you, but I've just spoken to Magistrate Mathias Robertson, and he is on his way to personally inspect the new facility. He's coming by train this evening."

All the color faded from Lucian's face. He pressed a button on his bracer, took a deep breath, and said, "Thank you, Murphy. Send his itinerary to my assistant. I'll greet him personally at the platform."

"I take it this is not a good visit?" Mira asked, not caring if the person on the com-link heard or not.

Lucian took another deep breath and shook his head. "We're going to have to cut this visit short."

Something had him seriously spooked, and from the sound of it, this new facility, whatever it was, was probably the cause. "What, no foreplay?"

That seemed to get a smile from him. Worried or not, he was still a man. Mention, or even just insinuate, sex and you had their full attention.

"Sorry, no. I know most patrons require special services, but that was not why I sponsored you. I do genuinely want to get to know you and learn the truth about your kind, and I hope you'll understand this sooner rather than later."

He did it again, saying things that made Mira want to trust him. "Well, then, I'll see myself out." She turned and headed for the door.

"Nice try. You know there are at least two guards posted to the other side of that door. You wouldn't make it ten steps."

"Can't blame a girl for trying. And for the record... I'd have at least made it to the lifts."

"I'm not a betting man, but I'd take that action." He smiled. Mira couldn't help but smile too. For a human, he really was attractive, and seemingly good-natured. He reminded her of Theo in that way. He'd had a disarming smile and infectious laugh once upon a time ago. "Let me cuff you and we'll send you off with your escort."

"Such a gentleman."

"I do try." He placed the silver cuffs around Mira's wrists and watched her curiously when she winced. "Do they hurt?"

"A little, but it's no real bother."

"You don't always have to act tough."

"Yes... I do!" She pressed the button on the side of the door to open it and found two guards armed with UV torches and semi-automatic rifles. "Hello, boys... ready to take me home?"

CHAPTER ELEVEN

T he cell door closed behind Mira with its usual clang followed by the mechanical clicking of the lock, but for once, Mira wasn't analyzing the sounds for clues on how to break free. Still a prisoner, still stuck in hell, but somehow at that moment, she was okay with it. Maybe she could trust Lucian. She didn't want to get her hopes up, but Lucian had mentioned getting her out. If he intended to help even in the slightest way, she might finally taste that freedom she so desperately desired. But the realist in her threw a wet blanket on those burgeoning hopes. Humans could not be trusted, a fact Mira had had beaten into her on more than one occasion. Nice words and some small comforts shouldn't turn her head so quickly. She needed to be smarter than that.

Mira stood idly in the center of her cell. To anyone looking, she might have been sleeping on her feet, but inside, she was silently warring with herself over how to feel.

"How did it go this time?" George asked?

"Why are you so nosy?" She hadn't meant it to come out so nasty, but he'd shaken her so abruptly from her thoughts she hardly recognized it was George and not one of the handlers.

"Mira, be nice." Unfazed by the hostility in Mira's voice, George had not lost his congenial tone.

"Sorry. Just... I don't know about this guy." She scooted close to the bars, wrapping her fingers around them, using the sting of the silver to ground her in reality. "He's not interested in me... in that way."

"Really?" His brow lifted. "What the hell are you doing up there?"

"Shhhh. Keep it down. He just wants to talk."

George's expression flashed between confusion and intrigue. "About?"

"Our kind."

"Vamps? Or gladiators?"

"How many non-vampire gladiator vampires have you met?"

"Right, I'm just confused. Why does he want to know about vampires?"

"I don't get it either. He seems completely clueless about how we live, what we're like, and what happens to us down here."

"Bullshit. He's a Regent."

Mira let go of the bars, her hands burning from the silver. She looked down at the angry red hives blistering her palms, a physical reminder of the truth – that humans were the ones who imprisoned her. "That's what I was thinking. He's an Elite. He has to have something... some ulterior motive."

George nodded. "So... what did you tell him?"

The blisters on her palms faded, but the lesson remained. "I told him every gory detail about the lightbox, training, and rations."

"Well, no wonder you didn't have to perform. You probably killed his mood." George laughed. "I know I wouldn't be able to get it up after all that talk of torture."

"I don't know. I bet the handlers would get a hard-on hearing all about torture."

"Touché!" George tipped his head. That was one thing Mira loved about her friend – he could always find the humor, even in the darkest of times. "So, your Patron... the Regent," he said with flair, "really just wanted to talk."

"Yeah." She didn't want to mention the part where he said he might be able to help her escape. George wouldn't believe it.

Mira still didn't believe it herself, but the inkling of hope remained, and she didn't need anyone to douse that small spark.

"Be careful, Mira."

"I hear you. He was the one who pulled me out of the arena schedule too. But I fixed that."

George shook his head. "I'd have stayed away from the arena if I were you. I heard the Magistrate is coming for this weekend's festivities. My Patron was pretty excited. The Magistrate is bringing his best fighters, too."

It shouldn't have, but the prospect of new fighters kind of excited her. Mira was known as the 'best of the best' in New Haven City, a title that had earned her a bit of animosity among the rest of the gladiators. She needed the chance to branch out a bit. Create some new enemies. "Good. I could use some fresh blood."

"Mira, you're crazy, girl!"

"Look, I'm either going to die and never have to endure another day here in the pit, or I am going to win and get fresh blood, something I desperately need. It's a win-win. That's better than rotting in my cell, waiting for the Regent to call me up for another chat."

"True… I guess. But if you have to languish in here waiting to chat with someone, at least it's someone worth waiting for. You know he's a man of power. It wouldn't hurt to keep him happy."

"Are you suggesting…"

"No. I'm trying to tell you in the nicest way possible that you need to do what it takes to keep this guy happy. Your reputation around here has got the humans wanting you dead just as much as your opponents."

"Let them come at me. All of them."

"See?"

"I'm supposed to be ashamed that I can kick all of their asses?"

"No, but you do flaunt it."

"I'm a survivor. I do what it takes, and I'm proud that I've lasted this long."

"I know. You're the shit! But at least consider having someone else, besides me, on your team. You could do with a few more friends… or at least allies."

Mira gave him a silent sidelong glance. She knew he was right, but she was not about to kowtow to a human, no matter how powerful he was. "I'll do what I always do… survive."

"I'm not really sure what that means, but I hope somewhere in that thick head of yours the message got through."

CHAPTER TWELVE

A **dusty brown tunic, belted it at the waist,** and flat leather sandals made up the entirety of Mira's pathetic fighting armor. Scantily clad though she was, Mira preferred to fight with next to nothing, even barefoot; but since this was a special fight, one which the Magistrate himself would be attending, fighters were required to wear full gear. This should prove interesting. She hadn't been in a fight with actual gear in quite some time. Her Owner had even sent her short sword out to be sharpened.

While she waited for her escorts to arrive, Mira wrapped her short hair into a bandana so no stray hairs would get into her eyes. With new fighters coming into the arena, she needed to be sure she had nothing impeding her vision. Mira was ready, almost itching for a fight. The rumor flying around the cell block was that the Magistrate had brought along his best fighters. Not much in the way of news made it into the depths of the Iron Gate prisons, but Mira had heard about a fighter called Mitchell. He was supposedly built like a tank, a former vampire resistance fighter, combat-trained – and, like she, an undefeated champion. He'd definitely make for an interesting opponent. One who might actually stand a chance of beating her.

Though she did not have a death wish, she'd welcome the end of this existence if that was the end result of her next battle in the arena. She'd lived this life for so long that nothing really mattered. Only the prospect of escape kept her going, and each attempt so far had been a disaster.

At least if she went out, she'd have an honorable death. Go out fighting. A warrior's death.

The heavy footfall of boots on concrete told Mira that her handlers were on their way.

"Ready when you are," Mira casually said, and stuck her hands through the bars.

The male handler led the way to her cell. Mira could tell him only by his height. Both he and the female were wearing head to toe gear again, including helmets with face masks.

They really must fear me, Mira mused, the thought bringing a smile to her face.

The male handler banged his UV torch against the bars. "Ready to die, slave? I'll be glad to be rid of you," he said. "Step back. Keep your hands in plain sight. No funny business."

While the male handler went to enter the code, the other pointed her UV torch directly at Mira, ready with an itchy-looking trigger finger, to blast her with a face full of burning light.

"I wouldn't dream of funny business. It's an arena day," Mira said innocently. She flashed her fangs and waggled an eyebrow at the female handler. She couldn't see the reaction, but felt satisfied she'd successfully made her cringe.

The male finished punching in the code. Based on the sound, Mira knew it had been changed yet again. Damn them. They must have her on a daily code change. That would make any future escape attempts a bit tricky. The lock clicked and the door swung open.

"Let's do this!" Mira held out her hands, awaiting the silver accessories to her fighting ensemble.

She gave them no struggle, and to her great credit, she even remained pleasant through their snide comments, rude shoves, and barked orders as they escorted her from her cell.

Normally gloomy and foreboding, the waiting area, affectionately known as the stable, was alive with action. A large hall of a room, lit with overhead fluorescent lights and filled with benches, the stable also held an extensive weapons closet guarded by a set of handlers. They were particularly attentive to any vampire coming too close before their time to check out a weapon. She entered the stable and took a spot at the nearest bench.

Mira spied quite a few new faces among the crowd of waiting champions. They all looked as if they were hiding their fears, but there was a palpable feeling of anxiety in the room. Everyone, Mira included, knew that these fights were often to the death, and not all the vampires in this room were as ready as she to see what Fate had in store for them. Anyone in this room could be Mira's end or a life she would be forced to end. The uncertainty, especially with new fighters in the room, was enough to give even the toughest fighter a moment's pause.

Three new faces caught her attention. Males. They sat together on a wooden bench along the far wall, their hulking forms barely covered by the fancy dark leather tunics that made them stand out against the rest of the Iron Gate gladiators. Even a decorated winner as she was, Mira had never worn anything more than a leather belt for armor. These men had much nicer and better protective clothing than anything the Iron Gate provided. Two of the new men were bald, recently shaved by the looks of it, but the third had a full head of golden waves. Though he was muscular, he looked too pretty to be in the arena. Surely he had a Patron or three who kept him busy. Maybe they were the ones to provide such nice armor. Mira spotted nice leather bracers around the wrists of the pretty male. His boots, too, were fancier than anything she'd ever see a gladiator wear. He had to be the champ – the one she'd heard rumors was going to be in this weekend's battles.

He caught sight of Mira staring at him and gave her a nod.

Mira returned the gesture. He looked like a Mitchell, she thought. The others seemed more like bruisers. She'd find out soon enough.

A human male with two guards at his back addressed the room. "Magistrate Mathias Robertson is in attendance today. He expects a good show from you all. Fights will be, as usual, to the blood, with final kill to be determined by his lordship, Magistrate

Robertson. You've been pre-assigned opponents. When I call your name, you'll take opposite sides of the room. Line up."

He began to list off names. New or unknown fighters always went first, followed by the regulars, and finally the known winners. "Mira to my left. Mitchell, to my right."

Just as she'd expected, the golden-haired man stood and walked to the other side of the room. Mira couldn't help but stare. Mitchell was just too pretty to be a fighter. But she'd heard he'd killed more than any other vampire. Despite his unassuming good looks, he was a merciless fighter, one not to be underestimated.

He noticed her scrutinizing him again and gave her another quiet smile. Rather than shy away from his gaze and admit she'd been caught staring, Mira kept her eyes locked onto his defiantly. She wondered if he knew of her reputation. Might he have concerns about fighting with her?

Somewhere deep within her, Mira knew this fight would be different. Trying to shove away her thoughts and focus on warming up, Mira turned away from Mitchell and began her stretching routine. With her wrists and legs still cuffed, her range of motion was limited, but she still managed to maneuver into a few positions. The gentle burn of muscles working helped to keep her mind riveted to the task at hand rather than on Mitchell and his surprising good looks and immaculate armor.

The paired groups went up. One by one they were called to fight. Mira heard the cheers of the crowd and smelled the tantalizing scent of fresh blood being spilled. Occasionally the fighters would return, some as pairs and some just single victors. Survival in the arena was not always based on being the best fighter. Sometimes the crowd picked a favorite based on performance and showmanship. Entertain the masses and you could save your skin. More than once Mira had been prevented from killing a felled opponent because the crowd called for them to live.

Finally, last in line, Mira and Mitchell were called up to fight. Mira approached the handler in charge of the weapons closet and requested her sword. As her hands were still cuffed, the handler retrieved her weapon, checked it off his list, and walked around Mira, sheathing it in her belt for her.

Mitchell was handed a rather odd-looking weapon, one Mira had never actually seen in live combat before. An ancient and nasty-looking thing: a ball with long spikes on a short chain attached to a wooden handle. She'd seen flails like this before in books, but never actually met a fighter who used one. Unlike his armor, this weapon appeared to have been used quite often. Based on the wear and tear, it was his weapon of choice. Some of the spikes had been sheared off, some worn to nubs. Deep scars ate into the wooden handle. Yes, this weapon had seen quite a lot of action in its time, and yet its Owner was as fresh and clean as if he'd never seen a day of battle. That, despite her resolve, gave Mira a moment's pause.

She suddenly wished she had a shield to use with her sword. But wishing would not make it happen. She shoved down her apprehension at the foreign and dangerous looking weapon. No good would come from showing her fear.

A gruff bark from her handler told Mira it was her time. She walked to the arena doors. Mitchell's name was called next, and he too walked toward the door. A cage dropped down around the two gladiators. Mira held out her hands toward the bars, waiting for her restraints to be removed. Her heart pounded with anticipation. Once those bars lifted, she'd need to be ready to fight.

Without a word of acknowledgement or glance of recognition to each other, Mitchell and Mira stood together while their handlers worked to remove their restraints. The front of the cage lifted as the doors to the arena opened.

The rowdy mass of spectators was still cheering the last combatants whose fight had just ended. Only one vampire would be returning to the stable alive. Adding insult to injury, the screams and howls of approval from the happy crowd as the other was dragged away by a team of handlers served to harden Mira's resolve. The poor wretch's blood muddied the ground where it had spilled and trailed on to another set of doors, ones only used to dispose of the dead.

The scent of freshly spilled blood caught in Mira's nose, awakening something primal within her. She'd recently been allowed extra rations, a gift of her Patron, to build strength before the fight, but nothing compared to the sweet smell of fresh, hot blood pouring from an open vein.

Mira and Mitchell entered the arena side by side, walking straight to the center. An announcer overhead called out their names, and the crowd erupted in another bout of loud screams, hoots, and cheers.

Mitchell smiled up to the crowd, turned around a full circle, and waved to his adoring audience. Mira remained still, staring straight ahead, caught off guard by the sight of her new Patron, Lucian, sitting next to the Magistrate. She'd seen him observing the games on many occasions, and watched for his signal to make the killing blow, but somehow, seeing him here, now, after their little chats felt different.

She nodded stiffly to the Elite box and then finally addressed the crowd. She held up her sword in a victory pose, and those in the crowd who were clearly her fans jumped to their feet. She may have been the bane of her handlers and owners, but the rest of the crowd loved her. She was a winner. She never failed to give a good fight. And she would not disappoint this time either.

"Combatants," the announcer called over the speakers. "It is your privilege today to be able to display your skills for not only your Regent but also our esteemed Magistrate. You may show your gratitude now."

Gratitude was not what Mira felt, but she'd done this so many times. She turned back towards the Elite box. "I fight for the honor of the Iron Gate and the pleasure of its people, and salute our great leader, Magistrate Mathias Robertson, for allowing me this opportunity."

Mitchell repeated a similar token of false gratitude. Mira could hear it in his voice; he was just as sick of this bullshit as she was. But that would not matter once the horn blared overhead, signaling the start of battle.

Mitchell's face hardened from bored to cold and calculating. He whipped his flail around overhead a few times in a nice display for the crowd.

The chain was no more than two feet, but she needed to account for the handle and his reach too if she wanted to stay out of striking distance. Her own short sword would not provide much protection. It was a close quarters weapon, and she doubted she would get the opportunity to get near him.

He swung it — more like flung it — at her, and she narrowly avoided the head of the spiked ball as it whizzed past her nose.

In unison, the crowd sucked in a deep audible breath.

Mira ducked the next swing but wasn't prepared for the recoil. Mitchell quickly backstroked with the weapon and whipped it back in Mira's direction. Even with her supernatural speed, she couldn't escape the blow. The spiked head of the flail came at her fast. She dropped her sword, reached out and snatched the ball mid-flight. A spike drove straight into her palm. She bit back a scream as she clamped her hand around the ball and jerked it back quickly. Mitchell held tight to the handle, overbalanced himself, and toppled down to the ground.

Mira, too, lost her footing. She released the weapon as she windmilled her arms in an effort to stay upright.

A mix of cheers and boos rained down from above. Clearly Mitchell had some fans. She would have smiled up at their taunting, but Mitchell was already bouncing back to his feet.

Her hand bleeding from her fresh wounds, Mira crouched, ready to strike. Mitchell was not giving her an opening; he immediately went to swinging the flail defensively. It whizzed through the air with deadly speed. Wicked fast with a supernatural speed equal to hers, Mitchell was damn near invincible with that weapon. She needed to get in close, but couldn't find a way to do it without feeling the sting of the spikes again. Her hand was bad enough. It was healing, but not as quickly as she would like. She could only imagine how pleasant it would feel to have those spikes pierce other parts of her body.

With her sword on the ground, she was completely defenseless. Her blade sat too far away, lying in the dirt just past Mitchell's feet. If she could get to it she might have a fighting chance. What she really needed was a shield, but that was not to be. She'd have to make do. Mira watched the way Mitchell swung back and forth, following the patterns of his arm. Finally, she saw her opening. As he finished his backswing, there, just a moment – but it was enough for her to get in close. She lunged forward, rushing him before he could bring the weapon forward again. Expecting him to go down with as much force as she had laid into her attack, she was shocked when she slammed into his body and he did not budge.

So much for knocking him out of the way so she could retrieve her weapon. Mitchell was immovable – all except for his arm, which snapped forward, carrying with it the flail. The spiked end of it wrapped around and hit her in the side.

Never before had she felt such an acute sensation. For a moment she felt as if the damn thing would slice her in two, the way the spiked head ripped through her flesh. The pain made her eyes water, but she did not cry out. She wouldn't give him or the crowd that satisfaction.

He flailed his arm again, ripping the spiked ball out of her. Mira had no time to lose; she ducked and threw herself to the ground.

She glanced up long enough to track Mitchell's movements and guess where his next strike would land. She quickly rolled left, then right, narrowly dodging the ball as it struck the dirt next to her head both times. Another quick roll to the left, and she scooped up her sword. She kept rolling a few more times, hoping to put a little distance between her and Mitchell's relentless assault with the flail.

It broke the air just inches above her face as Mitchell swiped low.

He was toying with her.

Mira righted herself and hopped up to her feet. If he wanted to play dirty, she'd play dirty. She held her sword up like a spear ready to toss. Mitchell halted, his stony scowling face contorted quizzically.

"You like to swing at things. Then swing at this." She jerked her hand forward but did not release the blade.

Mitchell however, began to swing his weapon. Mira took advantage of Mitchell's inability to stop the forward momentum of his arm and let loose her blade, throwing it like a spear. It hit Mitchell in the shoulder of his flail arm. Exactly what Mira wanted.

Mitchell held tight to his flail but his arm had gone limp. Blood began to soak through his tunic. The smell of it taunted Mira. She knew his essence would be her reward and looked forward to sampling it.

She gave Mitchell an impish smile. One she was surprised to see him return. With his good hand, Mitchell gripped the sword and yanked it from his arm. He dropped it to the ground at his feet and stepped on it.

Not the reaction she was hoping for. Lesser vamps would have conceded defeat and hoped for the leniency of the Regent to allow them to live to fight another day. Not Mitchell; he swapped the flail into his good hand and resumed his taunting barrage of swipes in front of his body.

Weaponless and without a plan, Mira bobbed and weaved, keeping herself loose and on the balls of her feet, ready to strike when she could. He'd make a mistake again, give her an opening, and this time she would not fail.

Above her and all around, the crowd was a roar of noise. Some cheering, some yelling to get on with the fight, and still others calling for death. Mira wasn't quite sure whose death exactly, but the humans clearly wanted blood.

Mira couldn't risk a look up at them or the fifty-foot screen displaying the fight; Mitchell's flail was already coming too close for comfort. Each swing pushed her back a half step. She'd expected his arm to have tired out, but that man had stamina she hadn't seen before. Even for a vampire, he was like a machine. Bastard must have had fresh blood before the fight, and not the meager rations she'd been given. She guessed he must have had a few pints, as energetic as he was.

Mitchell changed direction and backhanded the flail in a wide arc, nearly catching her in the side of the head. She knew he was baiting her, pushing her exactly where he wanted her. Through his stony face she caught something of a curiosity – the dead gaze of his golden eyes told her that he was not enjoying this. It was all business to him. Nothing personal. She recognized the look as it was one she often had while fighting an opponent she knew she would best.

That enraged her further. Not that she wanted to see Mitchell enjoying the fight, but that she was not worthy of his concern as a fighter. She was the best New Haven City had to offer! She deserved a little recognition.

Mira snarled, wanting to rip that damn weapon from his hand. Show him what kind of a fighter she really was. Maybe take the whole arm with it. But she just couldn't find a way in. He was relentless, creating a good six-foot barrier between himself and Mira, all while pushing her backwards. She understood now why he was such a renowned fighter. Who could get close to him? With his speed, stamina, and that weapon, he had all the advantage in hand-to-hand combat. Well, if she could get her sword, she'd have more to fight with than just her hands. She just needed a good opening.

Her sword now lay behind Mitchell; he'd advanced on her enough to have left it behind him. She watched the movement of his arm and the pattern to the direction of his flail. Knowing that he was weaker and less able to react in the moments before a backhanded stroke, she waited precisely for that moment to strike.

She bolted forward as Mitchell's hand finished its cross in front of his body. She twirled as she neared him, bumping him with her ass as she rotated. Hoping to knock him off balance she threw her weight into him. Without waiting to see if she had accomplished her goal, she continued to twirl and then ducked when she reached her sword.

The air broke above her head. She heard the fast whiz of the spiked ball, missing her by scant inches.

Damn, he was a quick one! As fast as she could, she grabbed her weapon and brought it up defensively and not a moment too soon. Mitchell had swung his flail again. It caught her blade. He yanked back, but Mira would not lose her weapon again. She held firm. The chain of the flail had wrapped tight around her sword. Mitchell yanked hard again, but Mira stood her ground, gripping the sword with both hands.

Finally the flail came free. Mitchell appeared to lose balance as his arm went back. Mira roundhouse kicked, aiming for his side, but caught him in the ass instead. Still, it was enough to send him, already off balance, toppling down to the ground. He fell in such a way that his body ended up covering his weapon. She'd hoped for the chance to grab it and show him a little of his own medicine, but she'd settle for kicking the shit out of him instead. She swung her foot hard again, and delivered a nasty, rib-cracking kick to his torso. He rolled over, bringing his weapon with him and tried to fling it with a wild backhanded stroke. She skipped back, away from the ball, and it landed in the dirt with a thud.

Mira stepped on the chain between the spiked head and the handle, still in Mitchell's arm. He tried to lift it, but strong as he was, he didn't have the leverage to move it this way.

She pointed her sword down at his face. "You're beaten. Call the fight."

"You know I cannot do that." He looked so much like he wanted to, but Mira knew better. She herself wouldn't have called for any reason. She'd die trying to win. And so, it appeared, would Mitchell. He rolled forward, toward Mira, toward her blade, impaling his shoulder upon it as he threw his bodyweight into her legs and kept rolling.

She was sent head over heels toppling to the ground. The hilt of her sword came up at her quickly as she somersaulted into the dirt.

When she was able to make out up from down, Mitchell had his weapon at the ready and struck. The spiked ball embedded itself into her left leg first. Then, before she could completely roll away from danger, it found the fleshy part of her right thigh.

She bit back the cries of agony that wanted to escape her throat. She didn't want to give the crowd that satisfaction. A third strike, though, made her bellow as hot salty tears flooded her vision. Her ribcage was shattered, or at least that was how it felt. Every nerve in her body had been sent the same signal: sharp, stinging, pain. She looked up, wanting to meet the eyes of her killer before he laid the final blow. But he was not looking down at her, nor was his weapon cocked and ready to deliver her death. Instead, he was gazing up at the Elite box.

The roaring crowd silenced. Tears blurred Mira's normally acute vision, but she did not need to see to know what was happening. Realization that she'd lost began to sink in. Her flawless record had been broken, like her body. She was unsure of what hurt worse, the sting of her pride or what felt like an endless wait for her death to be ordered.

"And now we come to the end of another glorious battle. Wasn't it exciting? What shall we do, my people?" The Magistrate's thick voice boomed over the loud speakers.

The answering response was not unanimous. Some screamed for death, while a few others, it sounded like, were calling for leniency.

"With great respect, Magistrate..." Mira heard the voice of her Patron over the loudspeaker. "She's our favorite here in Iron Gate. I think we should spare her for the sake of future entertainment."

The crowd cheered again. Some chanted Mira's name.

Mitchell turned his head down toward hers. She blinked away the tears, but they would soon be back. Every ounce of her being was on fire.

"I'm glad to spare you," Mitchell whispered. "You're my favorite as well."

"Thank you." It was all she could manage to say. She was done, body spent. They might as well kill her. With the little rations she'd be given, it would take weeks to heal properly.

Weak and beaten as she was, Mira was glad the fight was over. She closed her eyes and let unconsciousness claim her body. If she woke up again, she'd deal with the aftermath of failure then. For now, peace.

CHAPTER THIRTEEN

Mira awoke with a start, expecting the cold darkness of her cell, but found harsh lights glaring down at her. She'd never been in such a bright and sterile-smelling room before, but she could guess at its purpose. Had she really been hurt badly enough that she required medical assistance, instead of just sleeping off her wounds? No, certainly not. She was a vampire. Nothing short of losing her head would permanently harm her.

"Regent, she's waking up!" a soft yet frantic female voice called out above Mira.

She tried to turn her head, but a hard, thick metal barrier prevented her from turning in any direction.

"What?" Lucian responded, but she couldn't quite gauge where he was in the room. "Her body must be metabolizing the drugs faster than we can administer them. Bring me another round of sedatives... now."

Weak muscles made Mira feel as if her body had been submerged in quicksand. Every small movement seemed to pull her further down into a dark abyss, but still she tried, futilely, to rise. Through the blessed numbness brought on by the drugs they'd given her Mira still felt the annoying sting of silver around her wrists. She tried to move her arms, to break free of the restraints, but couldn't overcome the weight of her exhaustion and sedative medication. Looking down, Mira tried to focus on what she could, looking for some way to escape. Her entire hand up to her elbow was trapped inside a large cylindrical cage. A tube, either red or filled with her blood —Mira couldn't quite tell— ran up from her wrist toward the ceiling. There it disappeared, probably into another medical room above. But why? What were they doing to her? Was this what happened to those who lost in the arena? And why was her Patron, of all people, standing above her with a clipboard, wearing purple medical scrubs?

"Relax, Mira, everything will be okay." Lucian's voice was chipper, a little too much so for the circumstances. She'd no doubt lost him and her Owner quite a bit of money in that fight. Perhaps this was a new form of punishment and he was happy to see it in action. If that was the case, she'd much rather take her final death. The humiliation of losing was already more than she wanted to bear.

"No, no. Don't try to get up," he said.

"Not that I could if I wanted to." Her throat dry, Mira's voice was barely a raspy breath.

"No. I doubt that you could. Even so, save your strength. You've lost a lot of blood."

"Then why are you taking more?"

Lucian bent down low, inches from Mira's face. "You're going to have to trust me. Whatever you hear, hold your tongue. I'll explain later." His tone brooked no arguments, and Mira understood that.

But why was he warning her? That man was more of a puzzle every time she saw him. Where he should have been livid at her for losing, he sounded calm. Where he should have ordered her to be quiet for asking too many questions, he simply told her to wait. And most of all, why did he lobby for her to live when she had clearly been defeated, disgraced in that last battle?

She nodded, wondering what was in store for her next. Having never lost a battle before, she could only assume the fun that awaited her.

A door opened somewhere to her left, and the whole feel of the room changed. Even without seeing what was happening around her, Mira picked up on the sudden anxious shift of everyone in the room.

Lucian stood suddenly and folded his arms behind his back. Mira smelled the new arrival before he spoke. His odor was that of one who had bathed in the sewer and then tried to cover the stench with a variety of citrus scents. The effect only served to give him a sour milk stench. How no one else in the room picked up on it, she did not know. Even with their weak sense of smell, the other humans in the room should have been repulsed, but no one showed any signs of it. That could only mean one thing – this newcomer was a man of great power, as was also evidenced by the stiffness in her patron's posture.

"Magistrate," Lucian said with a salute, beating his left shoulder three times with his right hand, then held it out in greeting. The Magistrate slowly took the offered hand and gave it a quick two-pump shake. Lucian continued. "As you can see, she survived. Her wounds are healing, slower than we had anticipated, but not out of the question, considering the blood loss."

"And how much have you collected?" The Magistrate's voice was thick, much like his body. The stench of him made Mira want to puke, and again she wondered how those around her were able to hold their gag reflex.

Lucian smiled congenially. "We're taking it slow. Only two pints today. We encountered a slight problem with the dosages of anesthesia required to sedate the patient but not taint the sample we're collecting."

Cold unfeeling eyes gazed down on her disdainfully. Clearly Magistrate Mathias had no love for her kind, but the disgusted look he gave her told Mira that he wished he could have had her executed. "You should have had this sorted out before my arrival."

"I've had my best scientists and doctors on this for weeks, sir. I have personally overseen every aspect of this project to ensure…."

Now she knew why Lucian was so interested in learning more about her and vampire kind. Anger welled within her, but she lacked the strength to act on it. It all made sense. Medical experimentation. A fate worse than death. She should have killed him that first day she met him. She'd be dead, sure, but so would he – and his experiments.

"I don't need excuses, Stavros. I need results… now!" Magistrate Mathias slammed his meaty fist down on the side of her bed.

"Yes, of course, sir. If you'll just have a look…"

"We'll need at least five before we can begin the first trial, am I correct?"

"Yes. And then we'll need another five to transfuse during the experiment."

"Then get me ten pints. How hard can that be?"

Mira's eyes went wide in shock. What the hell were they going to do with her blood?

"Understood. But, we cannot bleed her dry if you wish for a successful outcome." Lucian sounded almost concerned about Mira's safety, but surely that couldn't be the case. Not with the Magistrate breathing down his neck. No. His concern was for his own skin. And apparently, that was in jeopardy.

"You should have had the initial collection done before I arrived." The Magistrate sounded more than annoyed. His spittle flew and he jabbed a sausage-like finger toward Lucian. "I don't wish to stay here any longer than I have to. "

"Sir, yes, I do apologize," Lucian was practically tripping over himself to calm the Magistrate down. "But you must understand, vampire blood is volatile. It only remains stable for so long. It must be used immediately. After our last candidate failed to withstand the collection, we decided Mira was the best candidate for this experiment. She is strong and vital. You'll see. Her blood will prove worthwhile."

If he hadn't been selling her qualities for his experiment, Mira might have been happy to see him come to her defense. As it was, she knew whatever it was he was selling, she didn't want to be a part of it. Not that she had a choice.

Unimpressed, the Magistrate shot a deadly glare at Mira. "She's a loser whose head should be adorning the spikes at the entrance of the arena."

"With all due respect—"

"Don't think I am ignorant to the fact that she is your play thing."

"That's not why I am—"

"Silence. Increase collection. I want the trial started tonight." The Magistrate turned around and headed back the direction he had come from.

Mira was glad to hear the fading footsteps; if he'd stayed any longer the stench alone might have done her in. Though, from the sound of things, that was exactly what was in store for her.

Lucian looked down at Mira, his face filled with sadness and regret. "I'm sorry, Mira."

"You say that like someone about to pronounce my death sentence."

"I may have."

"Go on, then, kill me. Make it quick, though. Slit my throat and let me bleed out. Quit toying with me."

"I told you – whatever you heard, you must trust me." He lowered himself and whispered. "I know how bad this all sounds. I cannot imagine what must be running through your mind. It is bad, yes, but my motives are not."

"Can you tell me what the hell is happening?"

He put his hand over her mouth. "Shhhh. Not so loud. It's best we keep things quiet until I can talk with you privately. Too many ears around."

When were there not too many ears around? Privacy was not a luxury anyone could afford. "So, what then? You drain me dry and hope I live?"

The nurse returned with a tray of what must have been the meds Lucian had ordered. She quietly set it down and turned to leave.

Lucian looked at the chart in his hand and sighed. "I will do all I can for you. But you have to understand I am under scrutiny."

Oh, sure. Her life was hanging in the balance, but she had to understand his position. The audacity of it enraged her further.

Good intentions or not, he was still treating her like a lesser creature. Hardly endearing, and definitely not a way to earn her trust – but Mira had no choice but to endure.

She caught the familiar clip-clop sound of stilettos on tile floor, heading in her direction. Great, just what she needed now. Of all the visitors to see her.

Lucian, however, did not appear to notice the new arrival. He had returned to scrutinizing his charts. Mira might not have seen her, but she could smell the familiar cloying perfume of her Owner.

"Getting friendly with the slave?" That shrill voice came from behind Lucian. "Patron or not, I will have my time with her. Do you know how much gold she lost me?"

Lucian turned on her with a speed Mira had not thought possible in a human. Gone from his posture was the worry and stress he'd shown in the presence of the Magistrate. He stood straight and tall as he addressed the pompous blonde. "Do not forget who you are talking to, Ms. Preston."

Mira couldn't see her, but she could hear the waver in her Owner's proud voice. "My apologies, Regent. I just… well… she lost me so much."

"She's under sanction from the Magistrate at the moment. When she has fulfilled her duty to him, you can have what remains."

The way he said that sent a chill down Mira's spine. If she endured this, whatever he had in store for her, she'd still have her Owner to deal with. And that rarely meant anything but a trip to the box.

"And if nothing remains?" Olivia sounded even more worried now. "What compensation will I be given?"

"If that's the case, we will deal with it then. Do not forget I have investments in this slave as well."

"Oh, I haven't forgotten. I trust she's been fulfilling her end of the bargain?"

"That is not your concern."

"I meant no disrespect, Regent. I only meant to know if she is keeping you satisfied. That is, after all, why you invested in her, was it not?"

"If that ever becomes an issue, you will be the first to know. Now, please leave, as I have more work to do with her for the Magistrate."

"Is she serving him as well? She looks to be enjoying her day at the spa."

"I assure you, ma'am, she is being adequately punished for her failure in the arena."

"Really? And what punishment is that?"

"Madam. I have been more than polite and tolerant of you, your disrespectful attitude, and your nosing about. You've been asked to leave once already. If you do not vacate the premises right now, I will have you forcibly removed." Lucian stepped aside and pointed to the door. For the first time, Mira was able to see the face of her Owner.

Mira had never thought it possible, but Olivia looked positively embarrassed. The red flush of her cheeks in particular caught Mira's notice. Blood. Something she desperately needed. She could feel it now, the burning sensation as her blood was being forcibly removed. The medication they had given her to numb the pain must have run its course and now the torture of empty veins was making itself known. A slow, burning hunger crept up her throat. She stared at her Owner, still standing defiantly in front of Lucian, with her heart pounding with rage. The frantic thump-thump of it called out to Mira like a siren. She'd lost so much blood already. It had to be replaced somehow. Licking her parched lips, she let out a slight whimper.

That small noise was enough to catch the attention of her patron and Owner. They both looked down at her with horror. Mira could only imagine the sight she must be. Eyes wide with bloodlust, locked on to the pulsing artery at the side of her Owner's creamy neck. Fangs bared, ready to strike, even though she had no means to do it. Strapped down to the hospital bed, she was incapable of moving more than an inch in any direction.

But still she tried, whimpering and grunting with need. She'd go mad with hunger if they waited too long to give her rations.

She struggled futilely against the restraints, finding them aggravatingly immovable.

"What is she doing?" Her Owner sounded shocked.

"She's being tortured in the most painful way possible. Leave... for your own safety."

"Please send word when it will be my turn." She turned on her extremely high heels and walked away at a pace much quicker than normal.

Gnawing hunger made Mira more beast than beauty. She no longer cared where the blood came from, she'd rip open any vein she could find and drown in the rushing waves of it. Like a caged beast, Mira pulled once more against her restraints, failing to budge them at all.

"Easy now, girl. I know what you need. Open up."

Mira did, baring her fangs and locking onto Lucian's eyes with a glare that screamed death.

Lucian uncorked a deep red vial and emptied the contents down into Mira's awaiting mouth. As little as it was, Mira savored it, holding the blood in her mouth for a few moments, letting it wash over her tongue and hit every taste bud. It was rat blood, and old at that. Some small coagulated bits floated around, and the consistency was that of warm jello, but it was still better than nothing. She swallowed and opened wide for more.

Lucian followed one vial with another, until Mira had downed at least twenty of them. Still her hunger remained.

"I can't give you too much at a time. People will get suspicious," Lucian said. There was genuine concern in his tone. "But I'll do my best to sneak in extras when I can. We need to get about ten pints from you today."

"Why?" Still ravenous, she barely recognized her own voice.

"I wish I could tell you right now. But I cannot. You're just going to have to trust me."

"You say that a lot, you know?"

"And yet you continue to question me and my motives. Have I not proven to you yet that I am not trying to harm you?"

"The blood you're stealing from my veins would say otherwise."

"At least you are alive for that blood to be taken. The Magistrate wanted you dead."

"At least I would have earned a warrior's death."

His brow furrowed with sadness, or maybe disappointment, at the mention of death. Almost as if he might truly care if that was the end Mira found. She wanted to believe that might be the case, but she couldn't trust him or his motives; at least, not fully.

"Death is not the answer," he said.

"Neither is slavery…. or medical experimentation."

"We can go round in circles later. I'm going to sedate you for the time being to help ease your pain and hunger. When you have recovered, we will talk." Lucian held up a syringe filled with clear liquid. "This might hurt a bit."

The ridiculousness of his words made her want to laugh. After all the things done to her, he was worried about a little prick causing her pain. If she'd had the strength she might have uttered a chuckle, but before Mira could open her mouth, a strange warmth overtook her body.

CHAPTER FOURTEEN

Heavy, as if they'd been covered by a lead blanket, Mira's limbs would not move. The drugs had worked to immobilize her, but Mira remained conscious, trapped within herself, experiencing the most unbearable hell she'd ever been through. Hours passed in an agony that she could neither vocalize nor fight against. She felt every drop of blood slowly leaving her parched body. Her veins burned. Deflating under the siphoning pull of the machines stealing her essence, her skin pulled taut against her bones. Each labored breath she took whistled past her parched lips. She couldn't imagine there was any more blood left in her body, and still they found more to take.

Her only respite came the few times Lucian came to check on her. Sneaking in a few extra rations, he tipped them quickly down her throat. Each one was like a moment of pure bliss, but not nearly enough to sate the burning need for more.

He'd joked to her Owner, that she'd be punished, and so she was, in the worst way. Mira would have begged for death if she'd had the voice or the strength to push air past her vocal cords. If it weren't for the involuntary dry rasping gasp, she wouldn't have breathed at all.

Mira didn't know how long she had endured. She had no way to measure the time, but eventually Lucian returned and, along with delivering her rations, he thankfully shut off the machines. Mira felt the agonizing pull against her veins stop. If she'd had the ability, she'd have moaned with relief.

With almost loving care, Lucian retracted the needles and pulled the tubes away from her wrists. Human or not, Mira was filled with thankful admiration for her patron. At that moment, he was her savior. And she hoped that he was here to end her suffering.

"I'm so very sorry, Mira." The way he spoke had the somber tone of one saying a final goodbye.

Did she really look that bad? Or was he about to start another round of torture?

Mira attempted to make a noise. But parched as she was, all she could manage was a rasp of air, just enough though to let Lucian know she was still there.

His eyes lit up. "Good girl. Keep fighting the good fight. I'll be right back with some rations."

That was music to her ears. Blood would solve all her problems. She'd heal, she'd be able to metabolize the drugs and overcome their effects, and most importantly, she'd survive.

Lucian returned with a few vials in his hand. Not as much as she was hoping for, but anything would do about now.

He tipped them one by one into her mouth and waited for her to swallow. "You looked like death had already taken you."

Was that sincerity in his voice? Mira continued to be bewildered by that man. She needed answers. Real ones... soon.

Cold, stale blood filled her mouth, and desperate as she was, it was better than anything she'd ever tasted. Awakening with revitalizing energy, her body began to repair itself.

Even after all these years as a vampire, Mira was still surprised at exactly how fast blood could help her heal.

As if she was coming out of a thick fog, her head cleared and her senses returned to their normally heightened state. She twitched her pinky toe, then her foot. Her fingers wiggled, and she felt the weight slowly lifting away from her heavy limbs.

"I'm a vampire. Death already had its chance with me once and lost," Mira rasped.

"Still a smart mouth, eh. Glad to see your spirit has not been broken."

"You can break everything else, but my spirit... never."

He tipped the last vial down her throat and Mira swallowed fast, instantly regretting her gluttony. Far from sated, she'd not even allowed herself to savor the sweet life-giving essence he'd smuggled in for her.

"Take it easy. I'm going to order you on rest for the next two days before I return you to your Owner."

"You'd be better off killing me here. She'll let me rest in the lightbox for those two days." Mira twisted her head from side to side, testing her mobility. Not quite back up to speed, but she was much better than she'd been even moments before. "Got any more rations?"

"Sorry, no. I'll order you some, though. Just be patient." Lucian worked to loosen the straps at her arms and legs. He left them on, but no longer biting into her skin. "As for Olivia... she'll not harm you further. Not if she wants to be paid."

"Paid?"

"For damages and lost time."

He spoke so matter-of-factly. It enraged Mira, constantly being reminded of just how little she mattered as a slave. Her life or death was nothing more than a monetary transaction.

"Really? Is that what you call this?"

"You won't make the next games because of time spent here, under the Magistrate's order. Naturally, your Owner will be refunded any portion of entry fees paid for the games and compensated for time you've been unable to perform."

"Really? I'm just a thing to you people, aren't I?"

"I don't mean it like that. This is just the business end of things."

"And our little arrangement? How much does that cost you?"

Lucian looked around cautiously. "This is neither the time nor the place."

Mira knew she'd stepped over the line, but she had such a hard time reining herself in when it came to her slavery. She wasn't a person. She was nothing more than an item to be used for whatever purposes they saw fit.

"Well, when is the time and place? I want some answers."

"You want? Are you demanding answers of me, your Patron, and Regent?"

She couldn't tell by his tone. Was he serious? Was he mad? Or was he just mocking her? On edge and still in desperate for more blood, Mira was teetering on the edge of control as it was.

"You and I have a unique relationship, but that does not mean you should be disrespectful. I'll arrange for another meeting soon. For now, play nice and take a nap."

She got the message loud and clear this time and decided not to press the matter further.

An agonizing wail came from a nearby room. A cry that matched the way Mira had felt but had been unable to vocalize earlier. Male, by the sound of it. Probably younger, Mira guessed, based on the higher clear tone. The wail turned into a series of shouts and cries. Whoever it was, he was no doubt in extreme pain. Probably another vampire being tortured within an inch of his life. But why here, in a human medical facility?

Mira could see other people in the room—nurses, doctors, and even patients—craning their necks and giving each other quizzical looks.

"Do I dare ask what that was?" Mira knew she wouldn't get the truth, but she couldn't stop the question from leaving her lips. The man next door was making such a ruckus she wondered if they were killing him.

Lucian's shoulders slumped. He let out a defeated sigh. When he met her eyes, there was no arrogance, only sorrow. "Phase two of our little experiment, I'm afraid."

More than a little shocked, Mira's jaw dropped at his honesty.

Then, a sudden and terrible realization hit her. She recognized the horror in those piteous moans coming from the other room. They were killing him in the worst way possible. It all made sense. They had stolen her blood. More than what would replace a human's blood supply. Had they, the humans, figured out the secrets of using vampire blood? Were they learning how to turn a human into a vampire?

"I am sorry, Mira. I need to check on this. Please, for my sake, and yours, just take it easy. Nap, rest, and recuperate. We will talk soon."

CHAPTER FIFTEEN

Dragged back down to the dank, dark prison wing, Mira was in no mood to antagonize her handlers or even attempt to decipher the code to her cell. She wanted nothing more than to just lie down on her mattress and sleep. She didn't even rise to their taunting comments or the hard jab in the back from a UV torch. She simply stepped forward into her cell and held out her hands to be unshackled.

"Finally broke her," the male handler taunted.

Mira shrugged and dropped to her mattress. Let them think she was broken, if it meant they would leave her to rest.

The handlers laughed as they walked away. As soon as they were out of earshot, George appeared at the cell bars.

"Mira, baby. I thought I'd never see you again!" The relief in George's voice was apparent, but Mira could barely lift her head to acknowledge him.

"You okay?" George asked.

"Yeah. I'm good. Just tired. Really, really tired."

"I can see that. What did they do to you after the fight?"

Where should she begin? "We've got to get the hell out of here!"

"You say that on a daily basis, babe," George laughed. "Can't be hurt all that bad if you're still plotting your escape."

"I'm serious, George. Bad things are happening. We need to get the hell out of here… all of us."

"Whoa. Calm yourself. Keep your voice down. What happened?"

"I think they figured it out."

"Figured what?"

"George, they took my blood. All of it."

George's jaw dropped. He let out a small noise, not quite an "oh," but close enough that Mira knew he understood.

"Maybe... maybe they just know of our healing properties. You know, topical uses."

"No... The way they were talking, it sounded like a transfusion. One to one. They took ten pints from me over the last... however long I was there."

"About two days total."

"It felt longer. I was drugged for most of it. Kept me still, but conscious."

"Poor thing." Horrorstruck, George looked as if his eyes were about to pop from their sockets. They gave you rations, right?"

"Some... yeah. Lucian brought them, but not nearly enough." She hoped he would keep his word and send her more rations. As much as she wanted to tell all, her conversation with George was already taking more energy than she had. Mira needed rest and blood, in whatever order they came. She wasn't going to remain conscious much longer.

"That man is really looking out for you. Did you see the way he stepped in at the games and stayed your execution?"

She remembered his swift work staying the Magistrate's order for her execution, but she'd have much rather he'd let it be done. The alternative was a fate worse than a quick death would have been. "Yeah," she scoffed. "So he could use me as his blood bag."

"Still, you could have been killed. That Mitchell guy was no joke."

It took all she had, but Mira lifted her head, shooting daggers with her eyes at George.

"Hey." George held up his hands in surrender. "Not saying you're a joke or anything, but that guy did have you dead to rights."

Mira hated to admit it, but she'd had no chance against Mitchell with that damn flail. "He fought well. I lost. End of story."

"It wasn't a fair fight, if you ask me."

"Thanks."

"So. If the humans are doing what you think they are doing—"

"They are!"

"What's your big plan? I mean, we're at their mercy as it is."

"I don't know. I haven't thought that far in advance. My head's still fuzzy. I just know we have to stop this. Think of what will happen if they succeed!"

"Total population control. We'd be even more expendable than we are now."

"Exactly!" Visions of uncontrollable carnage flashed in her mind. Vampire heads on spikes adorning every pike in the arena, piles of dead vampires being dragged off through the *other* arena door, the one for losers in the arena, and the dirt of the arena stained permanently red with spilled blood. "You think we have it bad now. Just wait. It can get so much worse."

"So, what do we do?"

"I wish I knew. I wish..." Her head hurt. Thinking required too much brain power. "Wait. I need to talk to Lucian. Maybe..."

"A human is not the answer to our human problem."

"Probably not, but I have nothing better to go on, and my head hurts too much to come up with something better."

"Is that you, Mira?" A loud male voice shouted from a nearby cell.

"She's here," George answered for her.

"Hey, Mira," the man taunted. "How's it feel to get put on your ass?"

That was all she needed. On top of the migraine and as tired as she was, now she had Tegan's gloating to deal with.

"Screw you, Tegan," Mira yelled.

"Everyone gets a taste of their own medicine once in a while," Tegan responded. "It's how you handle it that makes you a real warrior."

Shocked and a little surprised, Mira had not expected a seed of real wisdom from the hulking Neanderthal of a vampire.

"I hear ya. Still licking my wounds," she answered back.

"Live to fight another day," he shouted again, his voice sounding more congenial than taunting.

"Let's hope so."

"Losing might have been a good thing for you, you know." George said.

Was everyone happy to see her lose a battle? "Really? How?"

"Don't take this the wrong way, but you're a bit of an ass. And no one likes a cocky bastard. Especially one who never gets their comeuppance. You walk around here like your shit don't stink."

She'd love to wipe the smirk off of his face, but for now she settled for giving George a 'shut the hell up' glare.

George's smile faded. "Other people think this. Not me."

"And what exactly is your point?"

"Well...this time, you got a taste of defeat, and you're being cool about it. That makes you likeable. People respect that."

"And you're saying this because..."

"It's always good to have friends."

"I have you..."

"You know I'm a lover, not a fighter."

"I think with the right motivation, you could be both."

"Let's hope we never have to test that theory."

A loud clip-clop of heels on concrete ruined the otherwise perfect sentimental moment. Mira dreaded having to speak with her Owner. That woman infuriated her more than words could say.

"Have a good time at the spa?" she snipped at Mira.

"Oh, lovely. Had the works: hair, nails... you know how we girls love all the pampering." Mira's voice dripped with sarcasm.

"Cut the bullshit. What were they doing with you?"

"You mean besides punishing me for losing? Nothing." Mira wasn't about to let on that she knew more.

"And how did they go about that?"

"Chemical warfare." Damn, she was nosy!

"Meaning?"

"I don't know. Poison. Whatever it was, they fucked me up good. I can't even get up."

Mira hoped that would be enough to satisfy. She didn't want to let on that she was healthier than she looked, or that her Owner was being kept in the dark about what was really going on.

"I don't want to hear your crybaby excuses. I'd have you in the lightbox right now if it weren't for the fact that your Patron has requested you.

"Not sure I can get up to see him. I'm so weak."

"You'll get up and you'll serve him in whatever manner he wants. Do you understand me? You keep that man happy and satisfied with you."

"I can't do much without blood."

Her Owner huffed. "I'll have a ration sent down early. But it's coming out of your dinner supply."

"I appreciate your generosity."

"I'm certain you do." Her tone was dangerous, but Mira wasn't worried. Olivia might despise her and desire nothing more than to make Mira's life a living hell, but because of the money she earned, Olivia couldn't give up such a prize stallion as Mira. No matter how bad an attitude she had.

CHAPTER SIXTEEN

Eager to get some answers, Mira rushed though the prepping routine before meeting with her patron. Even cuffed and escorted, Mira managed to quicken everybody's pace up to the suite, and when the door opened and Lucian greeted her, she almost ran him down to get into the room.

"Someone is eager today," one of the handlers laughed as he uncuffed her hands and feet.

Mira smirked but did not rise to the taunt.

As soon as the door closed behind her handlers, Mira turned on Lucian. "You want to tell me what happened back there?"

"Well now, you've certainly gotten bold, haven't you?" His tone was a precarious balance of annoyance and amusement, but Mira wasn't in any mood to play the 'nice' game. She wanted answers... real ones.

"Don't screw with me."

His usually congenial smile turned hard. "And don't *you* take that tone with me. Helpful and tolerant as I have been, I am still Regent of this city."

The *power play* card, so like a human. "You nearly killed me."

"I did all I could to save you."

"You were the one in charge of the experiment."

"I was under the Magistrate's command. He was watching every move I made."

Passing blame, the oldest trick in the book. Lucian was certainly playing his part well. "That's no excuse. You damn near killed me."

"If it weren't for my stepping in on your behalf, you would be dead."

They could go round and round on that topic for hours, and Mira knew neither of them would relent. "Fine... what happened is in the past." She flopped down on the couch with a frustrated sigh. "Tell me. What did you do with my blood?" Mira really hoped that she did not know the answer to that question.

"We used it... on a patient."

"To heal them?" She arched an eyebrow.

"Not exactly."

"And the result?"

Lucian eyed her suspiciously. "Inconclusive. Why? Should he have healed?"

Mira shook her head in response, trying to keep her face neutral. She didn't want to let on that she knew what was happening. The humans hadn't learned how to use vampire blood. Thank the gods! They couldn't have done it right if the results weren't immediate.

Lucian joined Mira on the couch. He opened his mouth to speak, but no words came out. Mira saw the battle going on behind his eyes – the mental struggle between conscience and status. Finally, after a few moments, he said, "I'm going to be straight with you, Mira. I really do want you to trust me, and I know nothing short of total honesty is going to do it."

She hadn't expected him to say that. But still, she had to keep her guard up. Pleasantly surprised, though, she was glad he was trying.

Lucian took a slow breath, preparing himself to spill the big secret. "What I am about to tell you is going to make you mad. Justifiably so. But please, let me explain before you pass judgment on me."

The sincerity in his voice was almost off-putting. "Why do you care what I think?"

"Because you're not what I expected. You're not what I was raised to believe. And… if that is wrong, then…"

"Then you're going to feel like a royal dick for going along with things for all these years?"

"Eloquently put. Yes."

"It *is* a lie. When my kind came out in the open, we were not your enemies. It was you, and your people, who turned on us."

"That's not what our history books say, and no human is alive from that time period to say otherwise."

"And you've made sure any vampires that were old enough to remember were exterminated."

"Again… that is not what I was raised to believe. And that is why I care about you trusting me. You're proof of the lie."

Mira's bullshit meter was blaring in the back of her mind. He didn't care about her. He cared about appeasing his own conscience. "Okay, so what is it that you have to say that will make me mad?"

"It's no secret that the Magistrate loves the games."

"And so does the rest of the country."

"Regrettably so."

"Your point?"

"You vampires are a dying breed."

"Because you're making us kill each other."

"Well, when you're gone, more games will still be demanded…"

"So? Fight among yourselves."

"I agree. But…" Lucian appeared at a loss on how to continue.

Mira could see he knew the answer but didn't want to admit it, so she answered for him. "Humans just can't bear to watch humans get killed!"

Lucian's shoulders slumped. Uncharacteristic for a Regent. For a moment, Mira saw the vulnerable human behind the title and status. "They don't take it as well, no. So the Magistrate is introducing a new program to the Senate for approval. He's going to propose we turn prisoners in order to bolster the vampire population."

She'd known where things were heading before he said it, but to learn the extent of the plan was a whole new issue. Turning one or two humans was one thing – farming out prisons and creating cattle for the slaughter was just plain barbaric. And he, her Patron, the Regent of the city, had been going along with this plan the whole time? She wasn't sure what was more disturbing. "You can't be serious? How is that any different than humans killing humans?"

"New vampires are more savage. They would make for bloodier and more exciting battles…." He held up his hands fearfully. "The Magistrate's words, not mine!"

"That's what you were doing down in the prison that day. You thought you would check out the vampire stock and see who was fit for breeding?"

"No… well… not really. I wanted to see for myself what vampires were really like, how you live, that kind of thing."

"And, what did you see?"

"Never had I imagined it was so bad. And now to learn what you endure… I can't with good conscience let it continue."

She knew all of that 'trust me' stuff was bullshit. He didn't give a damn about her or her kind. He was just feeling guilty. But at least guilt was a starting point.

"So that's why my blood was taken. I was fit for breeding."

"I had to say something to prevent the Magistrate from having you executed. And your reputation for being a strong fighter helped."

Strength was only part of the equation, timing was the biggest part; but Mira was not about to let on. "You know, you humans have tried for years to get the secret of turning someone from us. Who told?"

"No one. We guessed that a full transfusion would work."

He was almost right. But it had to happen quickly. Mira assumed they tried to replace what they had taken over time. The tube leaving her body must have been going straight up to his.

What they'd done was worse than torture to that poor bastard. A botched turning was not a pretty sight. His body would have literally destroyed itself from the inside out.

"I'm guessing by the repulsion in your eyes that we did it wrong."

"Has the patient died yet?"

"Last I saw, no."

"Kill him."

"I can't."

"He won't live anyway, but whatever time he has left will be in pure agony."

"Why? What did we do wrong?"

"That, I cannot say. I don't really know," she lied. "But if you had done it right, he would have transformed quickly."

"So how do we fix it?"

"You don't. He's a dead man. It's just a matter of time."

"The Magistrate will not be happy."

"Poor him." Still worried about what the Magistrate wanted and how he felt over the pain and suffering of others. Lucian's heart might have been heading in the right direction, but he was still an Elite. He had no real concept of how bad things were. And she was not sure he ever would, either.

"I didn't mean it to sound like that. The Magistrate... he'll demand we do it again and again until we do it right. If I don't bring results, he'll find someone else to do it."

"You can't. You're not a vampire."

"Then will you do it?"

"That's it, isn't it? You want me to trust you so that you can use me as you see fit. No. Hell no. I'd rather die than create more slaves for you."

"That's not what I am asking."

"Then what?"

"Help me."

"To do what, exactly?"

"To put a stop to this craziness."

That was not what she had expected him to say.

"You're the Regent. Do something Regent-like."

"No matter what I do, I am still beholden to the Magistrate."

"Is that what you're asking me to do? Kill him?"

Lucian put a finger to his lips. "I never said that."

"You did understand that I do not like to have to kill. I do it because you all force me to. And this is how you want me to help solve that problem – more death?"

"If you have a better suggestion, I'm all ears."

The com-link on Lucian's bracer beeped softly. "If you'll excuse me a moment." He stood and walked towards the adjoining room to answer the call.

For the briefest of moments, Mira wondered if killing the Magistrate would actually be enough to stop the madness. Probably not. Humans loved the games. The way they packed in the arena each week to watch, the way they screamed for death… They were more bloodthirsty than she had ever been in all her years as a vampire, even those first few years when she'd felt she would never be sated. No. Simply killing the Magistrate wouldn't solve anything.

"Damn it!" Lucian yelled as he returned.

"I'm guessing the patient did not make it."

"You knew that would happen."

"Yes. I told you, you did it wrong."

"Then how do I do it right? Wait. You know what? I don't want to know. I never wanted to be part of this project in the first place."

"Easier said than done, I assume."

"You don't know the half of it. He's furious. And will take it out on both of us."

"Why you?"

"Because I failed." There was no hiding the desperation in his voice. Mira caught it quite clearly and it perplexed her even more.

"But you're the Regent. Surely…"

"I'm replaceable."

"So am I. Welcome to my world."

"You see now why killing him might be our only choice?"

"Sure. We could do that. But what about the rest of the people who love the games? Will they just suddenly decide that vampires are people too? Especially after one kills their leader?"

"No. Especially when you put it like that." Lucian's eyes spoke of the sheer desperation he was feeling far more than his words did. It was almost heartbreaking.

"I agree things need to change, but the how of it is the part we need to work on. Much as I would love to spill his blood, it has to be done in a way that does not implicate my kind further."

"Agreed."

"But I don't know how to go about it."

"We'll have to think quickly. He returns to the capital city when these games are finished."

"I do my best thinking on a full stomach." Not entirely true, but Mira wasn't going to pass up an opportunity to get a few more rations.

"Of course. I'll be sure to send down extra rations for you... so you can be at full strength for your next battle."

So much for her rest. She should have expected it, though. Rest was not a luxury she could afford, high-ranking Patron or not. "And when would this be?"

"Magistrate's order. You're to appear again in the arena tomorrow."

"And would I be facing the infamous Mitchell again?" Glutton for punishment as she was, Mira wouldn't mind another chance to prove herself against that warrior.

"No, he's already bested you. You'll fight someone more your speed."

Mira's gaze turned dark. "I'm not quite sure how to take that."

"From where I sit, it's a good thing. Easy win for you. But the Magistrate wants to shame you for losing."

"And that means?"

"An unfair fight of course... from his perspective. But I know your abilities. Weaponless and armorless, you can still beat this guy."

"I appreciate the vote of confidence, but the blood will do me more good than that."

"And what blood would suit you best?"

Dare she dream to taste what she truly desired? "Human. Hot, fresh, and straight from the vein."

She expected to see fear or revulsion in his eyes, but there was none. In fact, Mira had the sneaking suspicion that he might actually want her to drink from him. She decided to cut him off before he could say something so ridiculous.

"But... seeing as that is illegal here, and something I would never do to you, whatever you can scrounge up will be fine."

There was a hint of disappointment in his mossy eyes. They drooped slightly with sadness, yet his lips did not betray his feelings. Pulled tight over a clenched jaw, he appeared to be trying hard to remain neutral about the whole thing. "I'm sure I can come up with something suitable."

"Are we done here? Apparently I have training, if I'm to fight tomorrow."

"Be careful. Stay alive. And please, try not to get into trouble."

"Your concern is comforting."

Lucian led Mira to the door and placed the cuffs around her wrist. "We need to work together. I think you understand that. I cannot do anything for you if you're unwilling to work with me."

"I'll be on my best behavior." Mira gave him a toothy grin, flashing her sharp fangs.

"I'll bring you back here again soon."

The door opened and Mira's handlers, armed with UV torches, stood ready to receive her.

"Take me home boys!" Mira winked playfully. "Oh, sorry, one of you is a girl... I can never tell with those masks."

"Move it," the female handler grunted, and aimed her torch at Mira.

"Ta-ta, Regent. Let me know when you want seconds." Mira waved both her hands and headed down the hall to her cell.

CHAPTER SEVENTEEN

Mira walked slowly back towards her cell, casting sidelong glances at each of the other vampires imprisoned with her. Some she knew. Some she'd been jailed with for twenty-plus years and still didn't know their names. They were not in the same fighting class as she. And others she'd bested, but they'd been allowed to live. No matter who they were, they were all her kind. Vampires deserving of their freedom. Not cattle waiting for the slaughter. The thought of it sickened her. She herself was awaiting her fate in the next arena battle. Sure that the Magistrate had something special planned to shame her for her loss in the previous match as well as the failure of her blood in the experiment.

The idea of killing him was tempting, even if she hated to do it. And if she had the slightest inkling that it would do any good, she'd kill him in an instant. But even the death of that sorry sonofabitch would not aid her cause. Not while the rest of the human population felt as he did. There had to be a better way. Or at least some way to change things.

"Well?" George looked expectantly through the bars as she was tossed inside her cell.

"Well, what?" She didn't mean for it to come out so snippy, but her mood had turned sour.

George did a quick double-take to make sure the handlers were out of earshot. "Did you... talk to him?"

Mira hated the expectant look in George's eyes. Hated it because she had to crush that small inkling of hope he had. With a heavy sigh she said, "Yeah, he's not going to be much help. He doesn't like what's going on any more than we do. If you can believe that. But he's too far under the thumb to do anything about it."

"Oh." George's whole body seemed to slump. "And what about the experiment?"

"It's worse than what we were thinking. But it failed."

"Well, at least there's some good news. Wait… what do you mean, worse?"

Mira dropped her voice low. "Farming humans for new vampire stock. If their plan works, think of the never-ending carnage!"

Shock stole George's voice, but his thoughts were clearly written across his face.

"Yeah, that's how I feel too. I'm not giving up my plans for escape. I'm finding a way out. And I'm taking whoever I can with me. We all have to get out from under the humans' control."

"It's a fool's errand. We're all doomed."

"You're only saying that because no one has ever succeeded."

"Your optimism is refreshing, but face facts. You'll never do it. Not without inside help. And from the sound of things, even the Regent can't come up with a way to help you."

Mira flounced onto the old mattress on the floor. For all her skill in the arena, she was useless trapped inside the prison. Never a moment without guards threatening her with UV torches; never without someone's watchful eye on her. Even now, she was certain there were no less than two cameras monitoring the cells in her area. And then it struck her. She'd been so intent on fighting her way out of the system. "No… I don't need inside help."

"Sounds like you have something up your sleeve."

"If I were allowed to wear any." Mira laughed. "But I do have an idea. Not a good one, mind you, but better than nothing."

"And you're going to keep it a secret from your best friend over here."

"Exactly... so he doesn't try to talk me out of doing something stupid."

George shook his head. "I suppose it's for the best, but know I do not approve of whatever it is you have planned."

"Noted and forgotten. You can thank me when you're breathing fresh free air. Or forget me when I'm burned to death under the hot midday sun."

George let out a muffled growl of disapproval.

"Submission, inaction, apathy, and wishful thinking will never change things. We've tried all of those ideas. Now it's time for a new strategy."

"Don't get me wrong. I'm all for your freedom fighter crusade. I am. I just want to make sure you're around to enjoy the spoils of war with me."

"You're a good friend, George."

"And don't you forget it."

"How could I ever?"

CHAPTER EIGHTEEN

As the last fighter left in the stable, as usual, Mira waited to find out who her surprise opponent would be. She'd been brought out early and chained to a bench in the middle of the room to watch all of the other fighters come and go. Some had been heavily equipped, some wearing nothing but their linen tunics. It seemed today's fights were all about unexpected matches. Many of the vampires fighting had been from classes below her rank. And of the fights, none of the losers were spared. A pair of vampires would enter, but only one returned. Mira understood the same would be the result of her fight as well.

"No weapons today." The handler said as he removed the chain holding Mira to her seat.

"Sounds like fun," Mira smirked. She wished she could see the expression behind the helmet her handler wore, but she was sure he was smiling. No doubt he assumed she'd die today. Without a response, he led Mira to the arena door.

Tegan walked up beside her and the loading cage came down from the ceiling surrounding them.

Mira had not been given a weapon, but her opponent had. Things were not looking too good for her. The Magistrate had definitely stacked the deck on this fight.

"Hate to be the one to kill you," Tegan said, holding up his short sword.

"Hate to be the one to die," Mira responded, her voice monotone to conceal the swirling pit of emotions turning her stomach. She very well might die this time in the arena. Not from the fight, however. Tegan might have the upper hand, but she was the better fighter. No. Her worry came from the uncertainty of what she was about to do.

"Joking aside, I'm sorry. I may not like you, but you're a damn good fighter. I don't like being put in this position."

"Then don't be in this position."

"What's that supposed to mean?"

"No more talking!" the handler shouted, and butted Mira in the back with his UV torch.

"And what will you do if I continue?" Mira couldn't help herself. If she was about to die, she was not going to do it kowtowing to the humans.

Before her handler could reprimand her, the door to the arena opened. Light flooded into the waiting area, momentarily blinding Mira with its brightness. She shielded her eyes, and so did Tegan.

"Inside – now," the handler said as he shoved at Mira, forcing her into the arena.

Tegan strolled in unaided. He lifted his arms and greeted the crowd, who cheered and screamed his name.

Mira, not wishing to play into any of the bullshit, strolled into the center of the arena and awaited the start of the fight.

The crowd around cheered and jeered. It was hard for Mira to make out exactly what they wanted. It seemed many were upset that she was not acknowledging them, while others seemed eager to get on with the match.

Tegan joined her in the center of the arena. "What's the matter with you today? Why aren't you playing the part?"

"I'm done with this bullshit."

"You're only done when they say you're done, and you know how that ends."

"I thought we were supposed to be the bloodthirsty ones."

Tegan snickered. "True."

"Do me a favor. Whatever happens here today, remember that we do not deserve this. Keep that thought close to you and remind the others."

"Wow, I didn't take you for the sentimental type."

"I'm not. That message was not meant to make you feel bad for me. Feel it for yourself, and do something about it."

"As if I could."

"When the time comes, you might get your chance."

He might not have understood what she meant, but at that moment, Tegan looked as if he really wished he was not the one about to fight Mira.

A horn blared sounding the start of the match. The crowd roared, and Tegan dropped into a fighting stance, his expression turning from confusion to one of steely concentration. "Good luck," he said earnestly.

"You as well." Mira stepped back and took on her own stance.

Tegan swung his sword hard in her direction, sweeping it just past the side of Mira's shoulder – a warning shot, meant more to thrill the audience than cause any panic in Mira. She wouldn't have feared him anyway. She'd beaten Tegan on more than one occasion on the training grounds. She easily dodged his attacks and kept herself just out of reach, defending but not attacking.

The crowd eventually caught on and began booing and hissing her name.

"What the hell are you doing?" Tegan said with a sweep of his sword again.

"I'm not playing the game anymore. I'm done."

"Then you force me to kill you. You know I don't want to do that. Just play along. Give them a good show. The Magistrate will see, and you'll get to live."

"No. That's what they want." Mira dodged yet another swing of Tegan's sword. "I'm not a dancing monkey. And neither are you. Remember that."

The crowd's displeasure must have become apparent to the Magistrate, who had been eagerly watching, no doubt hoping to see Mira fall.

A horn sounded, and Tegan, like a trained dog, dropped his sword.

"Why does the female not fight?" The Magistrate asked over the loud speaker. "Does she not wish to give her adoring fans a good show?"

"No, she doesn't!" Mira shouted back. "And this female has a name."

"This female should remember who her benefactors are. Your kind are a plague upon this earth. We graciously allow you shelter and… rations. In exchange for that, you are expected to do your part."

"Funny how you call blood 'rations' when it's fed to us, but consider it 'sport' when you force us to spill it for your entertainment."

"How dare you speak to me like this!"

"Mira, what the hell? Do you truly have a death wish?" Tegan said under his breath. "Don't piss off the Magistrate."

Mira finally acknowledged the crowd. "You all seem to forget that we, vampires, were once human. We were born human. Like you."

"You creatures are nothing like us." Anger more than annoyance turned the Magistrate's voice to pure acid.

Mira knew she'd signed her own death warrant, but she hoped that her message would get through to the masses. She couldn't fight the system. She was never going to be able to overcome those unsurmountable odds, but if she could make the system change, her death would not be in vain. "No. We never killed for sport. We only took what we needed to survive, and even then we had no need to murder the innocent."

"Your kind are hardly innocent." In his anger, the Magistrate had turned a visible shade of plum. He almost matched his robes.

"Says the man hoping to create more of my kind."

A collective gasp filled the arena.

Mira looked up, finding the nearest camera and stared straight into its lens. Her face filled the fifty-foot big screen and no doubt every other screen in the Iron Gate province. Viewers here as well as at home would hear her message. "That's right. Your illustrious leader has been secretly working to learn the method to creating more of my kind to slake your bloodlust in the arena. You call us savages, bloodthirsty, and creatures, yet you don't blink an eye when watching our kind die each and every week here in the arena. Soon, he'll be able to turn any one of you, and then force you into the arena."

With a heavy breath, the Magistrate attempted to calm himself before speaking, but his tone proved he'd failed to do so. "I've heard enough of this creature's fear-mongering and lies."

Lights shot down from the ceiling above. Mira found herself caged in the burning light.

"A quick death is too easy for her. I want her staked out in the center of town for all to see. She'll burn in morning light."

Mira smiled wide. "I welcome my end. At least then I will have peace." Things were working according to plan so far. She only hoped the second half of her crazy secret plan would work as well. Her Patron, man of power that he was, should come to her rescue before she was devoured by the sun; but even if she did end up a pile of ash in the morning's light, at least she had gotten the message out. That alone should be enough to start the wheels of change in motion. Surely the rest of the human population wasn't that brainwashed or brain-dead.

Five handlers came to retrieve her from the light cage, each one bearing a UV torch ready to use at a moment's notice.

"Take me away, boys." Mira held out her hands to be cuffed without a fight.

Tegan looked on, utterly confused.

"Remember. Someday it will be your turn to do something," Mira said as she was led away from the arena.

The crowd was in complete disarray. Exactly what Mira hoped for. Some couldn't care less about the vampires' plight –

but others, people with a conscience, would begin to question their leadership. The seed had been sown.

CHAPTER NINETEEN

S tretched wide across a wooden table, arms and legs bound in thick silver chains, Mira was laid out like a beautiful offering to the sun. But her handlers were not finished with her yet.

To her left, she saw the sneering smile of her regular handler. She wished she knew his name, and more than that, she wished now she hadn't mouthed off so much to him. He looked positively thrilled as he held up a large silver-colored spike. With a heavy mallet, he drove the spike straight through her wrist.

Pain beyond reason flooded her body, but she dared not let out the scream threatening to explode from her throat. She would not give them that satisfaction. The second spike through her other wrist was harder to withstand, but again she bit back her cries of pain.

The third spike they drove straight into her chest. Not through her heart. No. They did not want to injure that organ and cause her to pass out; they wanted her to feel every moment of the punishment she had earned. In unbearable pain, she couldn't hold back the scream this time.

"Now, that's what I wanted to hear." The voice of the Magistrate preceded his stench for once. "You've caused me quite a bit of trouble. And in your arrogance, you thought you'd get away with it, didn't you?"

Even if Mira could have talked at that moment, she wouldn't have dared. There was no good in giving in to his goading.

"Fancy yourself a smart little vampire, eh? Thought you would incite a riot and escape in the confusion?"

He walked around her, admiring his minion's handiwork. "Spikes through the feet, too. I want her to be an amazing spectacle when we put her out in the town center for sunrise."

Mira braced herself for the pain that was about to come.

"If you vampires were half as smart as you think you are, you'd never have ended up as our slaves. If you cannot handle your lot in life, then you'll just have to be the example that keeps the others in line."

Mira felt her left leg being shifted and her foot being placed down onto the surface of the table. Moments later the spike pierced her skin and ran straight through her foot.

She couldn't hold back the cry. And as the second foot was nailed to the table, tears ran unchecked down the sides of her face.

"At least I will die knowing I did my part to change things." She spat the words at the Magistrate.

"No one will care about your death, or your parting words. You're just another vampire. But, come morning, you'll be a thrilling fireworks display."

Breathing through the agony, she spoke slowly, ensuring her words came out loud and clear. "Some care. And that look of fear you're trying to hide in your eyes tells me you know I'm right."

"A small problem. One that will soon be remedied." The Magistrate turned to one of the guards. "Bring in Lucian."

His was the last name Mira expected to hear.

Beaten and bloody, Lucian was brought in bound in irons, looking as if he were on death's door already.

"Ahh, Lucian, good of you to join us." He addressed his guard again. "Please find an appropriate place to put our former Regent."

"What's going on here?" Mira demanded. She'd actually hoped he'd be her savior. She'd counted on his status and position as Regent to ensure his safety and her own. Now it seemed both of them were going to be put to death, a fate she'd happily accept herself but not at the cost of his life, too. He was innocent…sort of. He'd helped her. He had told her of the Magistrate's plan. For all his attempts at good deeds, her actions had condemned him.

"Well, now, are we surprised to see our lover and informant?" The Magistrate laughed. "It has come to my attention, and will be made public knowledge, that our former Regent has been working on unethical experiments to try to increase the vampire population. This simply cannot happen. As Magistrate, it is my duty to punish such unlawful behavior and bring peace and safety to my people."

"And remove all links to your own involvement," Mira sneered. Everything, it seemed, had been all for naught. Both she and Lucian would be dead, and the Magistrate would spin new lies for the human population. Her stomach churned with the sour taste of failure and guilt.

"He's been sentenced to death right alongside of you, his cohort. When your body burns in the sun, he too will share in the experience. We'll have to help things along with a little fire of our own, but you shall both enjoy the same fitting end for your treason."

Lucian, barely conscious, grunted, but had no strength to struggle. He was secured to the rack alongside Mira.

"Wheel them out to the city center. I want cameras set up to catch the show come sunrise," the Magistrate said as he walked out of the room.

CHAPTER TWENTY

For the first time in years, Mira saw the stars. She hadn't been allowed outdoors since her capture. The fresh night air stung her already-ruined skin, but she welcomed its cold bite. Even the subtle scent of garbage clinging to the breeze was a welcome change from the musty dungeon air of her former prison. She savored each breath of unfiltered air, knowing they might well be her last.

The cart carrying her and Lucian stopped in what must have been the city center. Some men came out, handlers by the looks of them, too lightly armored to be regular soldiers. They made quick work of securing Mira and Lucian to their racks and connecting chains to the ground. The men unhitched the trailer that had been pulling them and drove away.

Silence, eerie and beautiful, surrounded them. Mira caught sight of a shooting star overhead. For all the beauty and magnificence of it, she could not enjoy it. She'd die not only a disgrace, but a failure too. Sacrificing her life and Lucian's for nothing. A foolhardy plan that had ultimately failed.

In a vain attempt to escape, Mira struggled against her restraints. The nails that had been driven through her limbs must have been coated in silver, as they burned relentlessly. For all her strength and willingness to rip off her own arm if necessary, she couldn't break free. She was well and truly screwed. There would be no hope of escape.

Lucian stirred. She heard him struggling against his restraints, but they'd been placed back to back, so she couldn't see him.

"You alive still?" she asked.

"Why?" His voice was barely a whisper, raspy and low.

"I'll take that as a yes."

"I asked for you to get rid of him. This was your plan?" Even through the pain, Mira could hear the disappointment in Lucian's voice.

"I told you simply killing him would not solve the problem."

"And getting ourselves killed would?"

She couldn't blame him for his contempt. "Minor oversight. But the seeds of discontent have been sown."

"And will be forgotten by morning."

"Nah. They'll remember for at least a day," Mira tried to joke, but deep down she knew Lucian was right. "Sorry to have involved you in this. I was supposed to be the only one to die."

"The Magistrate had his suspicions the moment he knew I was Patron to a vampire."

"And you didn't even get to take advantage of all a Patron enjoys."

"Oh... I'd say you fucked me pretty good here."

"Well, now, things can't be all bad if you're making jokes." Mira would have laughed if she weren't in so much pain it took all she had to hold back the tears.

"We'll see. Can you move at all?"

"I'm kind of tied up here. Oh and nailed to the table."

"Sorry. I hoped your vampire strength would help us out here."

"So did I. Got any brilliant ideas?"

"Maybe."

"That's reassuring."

"I may have been branded a traitor, but I still have a friend or two."

"Let's hope you do. Dawn will be here soon enough, and I am really not looking forward to death by sunburn."

The dull thud of a rock hitting dirt nearby caught Mira's attention. That was no random falling stone. It hit too closely and too precisely to have just dropped on its own. She listened carefully. Footsteps, slow and quiet were coming closer to her. Another rock hit the dirt nearby.

"Is that you, Death?" Lucian said as loudly as he could manage with his raspy voice.

Another male voice responded, "Come to deliver you to the gates of hell."

"Friends?" Mira whispered cautiously.

"Yes."

Two humans arrived clad all in black. At first glance they appeared to be handlers, but Mira's eyes were better than that. These two were no trained soldiers, nor were their clothes the sleek black of a handler's armor. Their clothes weren't even armor at all, Mira saw as they came closer. They were far too simple for any formal uniform: long-sleeved shirts and pants, with what appeared to be dark hats pull low to cover their eyes. A male, the one who had responded to Lucian, came forward first, followed by a female whose face was completely covered. It was only the hint of flowery perfume that gave her away. Without a word, she immediately went to work removing the large spikes.

They hurt Mira more on the way out than they had going in, but knowing that silence was their ally, she kept herself as quiet as she could, whimpering only when the pain became too great.

When all the spikes had been removed, the man pulled out a pair of bolt cutters and made quick work of cutting the chains shackling her to the table.

"Get up and get moving, quick!" The male barked the order at Mira. "We need to move now." He shouldered the limp form of Lucian, and together with the help of his female companion, headed into the shadows.

Weak and woozy, Mira took a moment to gain her balance. Wobbling on unsteady legs, she followed as best as she could behind them.

Following back alleyways, they slowly weaved their way through the city towards what appeared to Mira to be a heavily residential area. Completely lined with rowhouses, the street was part of a well-planned-out community. Street lights were uniformly set every four houses. A small walkway separated the street from the concrete steps up to each two-story brick home. In front of every house was a clearly marked parking spot labeled with the number of the home to which it corresponded. It was almost too perfectly laid out. Like her prison, only a little bit nicer. For all its perfection, it lacked something. Not a single blade of grass nor tree nor bush anywhere. Perhaps more like her prison than she had first thought. It might look prettier, but it was no more inviting.

Just then, she spotted a blinking red light under one of the street lights. On second glance, she saw it was a camera.

"We're being watched."

"Don't worry about the cameras right now," the male responded. "The streets aren't closely monitored. Those cameras are fixed. Just keep to the shadows and don't stop moving."

Expecting to be heading away from the city, Mira couldn't help but feel they were traveling further inside it. "Where are we going?"

"The sun will be up soon. We won't be able to clear the city walls before that happens. You'll stay with me today, and we'll make our escape this evening," the male called out behind him.

Not what she'd hoped to hear. Spending another day inside the city walls was a dangerous proposition. No doubt their absence would be noticed and a manhunt would ensue, making any future attempts to leave doubly hard. But as she had no other option, she soldiered on, following as close to them as she could manage in her injured state.

They ducked inside a small doorway just off the alleyway, which led down a set of stairs to a large basement.

It was small and filled with all manner of human junk: old clothing, boxes, and shelves of god-only-knows-what. What it didn't have, thankfully, were visible windows. It wasn't much but that one fact alone made it a perfect sanctuary. Mira took a moment to catch her breath and acknowledge her rescuers. "Thank you."

"No offense to you, vampire," the male responded. He pulled his hat off and met her gaze straight on. "We did not do this for you. We're loyal to our Regent."

Strong words for someone who appeared so frail. The man was older than she'd expected. He'd shouldered Lucian and carried him for the better part of four miles, so she'd expected to see a young, strapping man of twenty or so. The man in front of her had to be at least double that, with a head of graying hair and dusky eyes surrounded by a face filled with wrinkles.

"Of course." Mira nodded. "As am I."

That seemed to smooth out any remaining tension with the male, who managed a smile. The woman, however, kept her face covered and stood well behind her partner. Mira couldn't help but feel she was using him as a shield.

Mira acknowledged her with a nod. "Thank you as well. You may not trust my kind, but you have my word I am in your debt."

The woman refused to respond.

After a brief awkward silence among the four of them, the male spoke up. "You'll stay here for the day." He opened up a hidden doorway in what Mira thought had just been a cluttered wall. It led to another small empty chamber. "You should be well hidden in here. Just remember to be silent. Not a peep until I return."

The man helped a barely conscious Lucian into the small room. Mira stood by, waiting for him to exit before going in to the small chamber herself.

"And how will I know it's you at the door?" As if his scent would not give him away.

"I'll speak the word 'gladiator'."

With that, he ushered them inside and closed the door.

CHAPTER TWENTY-ONE

Mira lit a candle in the corner of the darkened chamber. As the light flooded the small room, Lucian grunted. Happy to see him somewhat alert, she sat down next to him. "So, do I ask how you orchestrated this?"

He adjusted his position, scooting up and leaning his back against the bare brick wall. "When I heard what you had said at the arena, I knew I would be taken into custody. The Magistrate had already commented on our… arrangement."

"So you had a lackey come rescue you?" She hadn't meant what she said to come out so bluntly.

"Don't you call him that! Curtis is a good friend and ally." The sudden vigor and aggression in his voice startled Mira.

"Well, by the looks of him, I would say he wasn't an Elite."

"No, but a better man you've never met."

"High praise."

"He's well worth it. He and his wife are risking everything by hiding us. You do realize that, don't you?"

"Why save me then, why not just yourself?"

"Because I care about you… your wellbeing, Mira. I put you in this position. I told you I wanted the Magistrate dead. I couldn't let you take the fall."

In all her years imprisoned in that damn place, she'd never been cared for. Not really. Sure, she'd been given enough care to keep her alive enough to perform in the arena, but that wasn't real care. Mira wasn't quite sure exactly how to feel about his revelation, let alone respond to Lucian's words.

She turned away, unable to look at him. "I was ready to meet my end."

"I know you were. And I would have been sad to see you go."

"You're a strange one, Lucian. Caring for a vampire." She knew it then; she could trust him. He'd more than earned it. Human though he was, he was not one of them, the bastards that had treated her so cruelly all her immortal life.

Lucian scooted up against the wall again, wincing as he moved.

"Are you badly hurt?"

"A few broken ribs, I'm sure, but nothing fatal."

"Maybe not now, but while we're on the run, you'll need to be at full health." Mira lifted her wrist to her mouth. Dried blood and healing scabs covered the spots where the spikes had been. Where the cuffs had slid up and down her skin, there were visible angry red hives. Still, though, she knew sharing her blood would help him. She could spare a few drops.

She bit into her wrist, hissing with pain as her teeth broke the skin, and then offered her blood to Lucian. "This will help you heal."

"No, I couldn't."

"Just a sip. Quickly now, before the wound seals itself."

Reluctantly, he took her offered wrist and put his mouth over the wound.

His tongue tickled her skin as he gingerly lapped at the wound. He grimaced, probably at the coppery flavor. Humans had no taste for blood. Why should they? Still, repulsed as she saw he was, Lucian did not pull away. He lightly suckled at the wound, swallowing a few small gulps before pushing her hand away, revulsion painted across his face.

"Thanks, I hope," he said, swallowing hard, trying to force down the last of the taste.

"It will help, trust me. Though you might want to lie down. You're bound to feel a little queasy."

He gripped his stomach and grimaced. "Thanks for the warning."

A gentle knock at the door caught their attention. Mira had not expected to hear from anyone until next nightfall.

"It's only me, gladiator," a male voice whispered. She recognized it as the man called Curtis.

Mira stood and opened the door.

Curtis entered with a small tray of food, bolt cutters, and some clean water and bandages. "It's not much at the moment, but this should help. The city is already abuzz with your escape. It's all over the news. Be sure to lie low and try not to make any noise, no matter what you hear. Only open this door if I or my wife speak the code word."

"Got it, thank you. Is there some way we can repay you?" Lucian asked.

"Seeing you out safely is repayment enough. You have a greater mission than I," Curtis said.

"Then it is not I you need to save, but Mira. She's the one with the mission." Lucian said.

"You both play your parts," Curtis replied, casting a quick glance at Mira before returning to Lucian. "And I will give my life to see you have the chance to play those parts."

"Let us hope it does not come to that," Lucian said.

"I'll be checking in on you when I can through the day. I'm afraid I cannot let you both out…"

"We appreciate your help and your protection. Thank you," Lucian said.

"I wish I could do more."

"You've already gone above and beyond," Lucian assured him.

Curtis nodded and turned toward the door. "I'll be back soon."

As soon as the lock clicked, Mira turned on Lucian. "Mission?"

"Just because the circumstances have changed does not mean I've given up on stopping the Magistrate." Lucian's voice had found its strength. Clearly her blood was working to mend him from the inside out.

"How exactly are we to do this on the run?"

"Once we're free and clear from the city, we'll have more time to plan. I don't have all the answers yet. Things haven't exactly worked out so far, have they?"

"That would be the understatement of the year. But I suppose we'd have a better chance killing him on the road than in the city. Still no guarantee we can pull it off."

"For now, our goal is to get out of the city and find some sanctuary to hole up in and regroup."

Sanctuary… Mira had long dreamed of finding sanctuary. It had been a place of legend when she and her group had sought it out, before her capture. Did it really and truly exist? Could she find it? The prospect of it was enticing. Yes, if they did manage to make it out of the city, she would certainly head in that direction.

"Mira?" Lucian sounded concerned.

"Yes, sorry. Just thinking."

"You looked as if you'd gone into a trance. What's on your mind?"

"Just wondering how we'll make it, that's all."

"One step at a time… but this time, let's be on the same page. No more of your half-baked ideas."

"Step one: You get some rest."

"Now, that's a plan I can agree with." Lucian's eyes were already half closed as he spoke.

CHAPTER TWENTY-TWO

Three small raps against the door woke Mira. A soft voice, barely a whisper, came from behind it. Curtis. "There's someone at our front door. Soldiers."

"Right." Mira's eyes flew open. Instantly she was on alert.

"You two lock the door from the inside, and remember – do not open unless the code word has been spoken."

Mira did as she was told, bolting the door shut behind him. Outside, she heard scraping sounds, as if something heavy were being slid in front of the door. She turned and gently shook Lucian, holding a hand over his mouth in case he made any sounds. When his eyes opened, she put a finger to her lips warning him to remain silent.

Moments later there were raised voices. "Sir, this is completely unnecessary. Who on earth would harbor a vampire?"

"Magistrate's orders. All houses are to be checked."

Not sure how much of this he was hearing, Mira gave a warning look to Lucian. "Don't make a sound. Don't even breathe."

Outside, the voices grew louder. Male voices. Deep. Angry. One, maybe two or more. "What's behind here?"

"More shelving and tools," Curtis answered.

"What did you say your trade was again, sir?"

"Electrical repair."

"And this? What does this do?"

"Nothing. Those are just internal components for an old-fashioned radio. I like to collect these old relics."

"Do you have a permit for that com-link?" The soldier sounded annoyed.

"I... Uh.. That's one I'm repairing." Curtis sounded scared.

"You're not permitted to have that level of equipment in a residence like this. I'm afraid I'll have to confiscate that and bring you in for questioning."

"That link is the property of the Elite's office. Confiscate it if you will, but be sure it ends up back there or there'll be hell to pay. The Regent requested that be fixed ASAP specifically."

"What do you know of the Regent?"

"Just what my bosses tell me. He wants something fixed ASAP, I fix it. I need my job, just like the rest of you."

"The Regent has been taken out of office, did you know that?"

"No sir, been hard at work all night trying to make this damn thing work. What happened?"

"Really, you have no idea what has been happening?"

"Sorry, sir. I don't have the money for a screen of my own. I get my information the old-fashioned way. Newsprint. And, well, the morning paper isn't out yet."

He sounded so convincing, Mira almost believed him. But something told her the soldier wasn't buying it. Not sure of what to do, Mira continued to listen at the door.

"Clueless or not, you'll relinquish that com-link," the soldier ordered.

"Of course, sir. Please take it. I'd hate to be tied into any of this bad business with the Regent."

"Smart man." The soldier's tone had turned from annoyed to almost friendly. "Don't let me catch you with unauthorized tech again."

"No, sir. I'll make sure my paperwork is in order for any take-home projects from now on."

Mira breathed a sigh of relief hearing the footsteps of the soldier going up the wooden steps.

"One minute." The soldier said. His footsteps halted on the stairs. "What is that light?"

Mira's heart stopped. She rushed to snuff out the candle.

"I have many lights down here. I need clear vision when I work," Curtis said.

"No. There was a crack in the wall and light behind it," the soldier said.

"These old places aren't built as well as your housing. I'm sure it was just sunlight on the outside of the wall, or maybe even the home next door's light."

"Out of my way." The soldier's footsteps came heavy down the stairs again.

"You ready for a fight?" Mira whispered to Lucian. "We're about to have company.

"Ready as I can be." Lucian stood.

"Stay a few feet behind me. It sounds like there's only one. I'll drag him in here and take care of him. If there are others, though, we might have a problem."

The sound of metal scraping against concrete told Mira the soldier had found the door. "Open this now."

Mira waited with bated breath. She didn't like having to kill, but this one was forcing the issue, and she needed the blood.

The soldier yanked the door open, but before he could utter a word Mira had him by the throat. She sank her fangs in deep and drank her fill. Hot, fresh, human blood. Such a delicacy. Mira had not savored that sweet nectar of life in ages. She gulped greedily, oblivious to the revulsion of those around her.

Nothing existed for that moment, just her and the soldier, his beating heart music to her ears. It pumped hard and fast – hot blood flooding into her waiting mouth.

Every ache, every pain erased. The heat from his fresh blood infused her body, restoring her strength and filling her with new vigor.

She barely heard the sounds of more footsteps coming down the stairs. The small click and charge-up sound of the UV torch should have immediately registered on her, but it wasn't until the full blast of white-hot light caught her straight in the face that she dropped her quarry.

Hands up to shield her eyes, Mira shrank back against the wall.

"Lucian Stavros, you are under arrest by order of the Magistrate," a new soldier called out. Mira couldn't see. The soldier kept the UV torch on full blast aimed right at her face. "Slave 8254-A, you are to be eliminated on sight."

"Thanks for the warning, but how do you expect to do all that?" Mira laughed. She couldn't help herself. She couldn't see him, but by the sound of it, there was only one person in the room. He had to be armed, but he was concentrating on keeping that torch on her face, which meant he couldn't grab for any other weapons. If she could just get past the pain, she'd be able take him.

"Silence, slave. You'll remain here until backup has arrived."

"You really think you'll live long enough to see your precious backup?" Shielding herself as best she could, Mira took a step forward.

"I said stay where you are!" The soldier held firm to his UV torch, but the warble in his voice told Mira she was correct. He was alone, and she could take him.

Mira's skin blistered under the harsh light. Small bits of skin flaked off, stinging and smelling of singed flesh. She'd dealt with this before, in the lightbox; knew this pain well. All she had to do was fight past it and she could have him by the throat.

"Lucian, are you up and moving?" Mira asked.

"Right here."

"Does the soldier have any weapons on you?"

"He has a small gun aimed at my chest, yes, and the torch in his other hand."

"Get behind me."

She felt the small breeze of his movement behind her. Hoping she'd be cover enough, she lunged forward blindly. A shot went off. Hot metal seared its way through her body, but that pain was minimal compared to the blistering heat of the UV torch. She met it dead on, flailing her arms to try to knock it out of the way. Her body collided with the soft yet taut flesh of a younger man. She hoped he was the soldier. They toppled down to the ground together. Baring her fangs, she sank them into the first bit of naked flesh she could find.

The soldier wailed with pain and struggled to get out from her grasp.

Mira locked on to him with all her might, wrapping her arms and legs around his body and rolling around on the floor with him, all the while keeping her teeth firmly entrenched in his hot flesh.

She gorged herself on more blood than she'd had in the last thirty years, savoring her gluttony. There would be no telling when she'd be able to enjoy such a bountiful feast again, and given her wounds, she needed the healing blood to keep her at full strength.

When she rose, Mira met the uneasy stares of Curtis, Lucian, and the obviously upset wife.

"Sarah, honey. Why don't you run back upstairs and get us some towels and things to clean this mess up, okay?" Curtis was visibly shaken, but still managed to meet Mira's eyes as he spoke to her. "Are you okay?"

"I'm fine. My wounds will heal fast. Are you and Lucian unharmed?"

Lucian knelt down beside Mira. Blood bloomed across his shirt, flowing out from the tip of his shoulder. "I'm okay. Just a scratch, I think."

"We better take a peek at it. Just in case." Mira turned to Curtis. "Have your wife get some first aid supplies."

"I'll see what we have," Curtis said, and headed back up the stairs.

"Hurry. We don't have much time. And if he did call for backup, they'll be here in moments."

"We have another problem too. The sun is still up." Lucian said.

"That's only a problem for me. You all can get out at any time," Mira said.

"No. We have to stick together."

"Not if separating keeps us alive."

"I won't hear of it. Separate, we are vulnerable. Together, we can use each other's resources to survive."

"Well, my resources are limited when daylight is involved, and as much as I would love to sit here and drink my fill, I can't keep killing soldiers all day. Think of my girlish figure."

"Did you actually attempt to be funny in your own snarky little way?" Lucian let out a snort of laughter.

"It happens occasionally."

Curtis returned with a small first aid kit. "We don't have much here. Hope some of it is useful."

Mira opened the small metal container. It had little more than a few bandages and a half-empty bottle of alcohol. "We'll just have to make do."

Lucian pulled off his shirt, wincing with pain where the fabric ripped at his skin.

"Looks bloody, but I don't think the bullet is in your shoulder."

"Just a scratch, then?"

"I'll need to clean it to be sure." Without hesitation, she dumped the bottle of alcohol onto his wound.

Lucian let out a howl of pain. Mira quickly silenced him with her hand across his mouth. "You want to alert the whole city?"

Panting with pain, Lucian replied, "Sorry, I wasn't prepared..."

"Just shut up." She inspected the wound. It bled like it would never stop, but she didn't see any type of fragments embedded inside.

"I'm not a warrior like you," Lucian said apologetically.

"I know." Mira had lived a life of pain. It was hard for her to understand that others might not have the same tolerance. "I'm going to give you more blood. I need you to heal quickly, okay?"

The expression on Lucian's face was one of deep revulsion, but he did not speak a word in protest. He took a deep breath, and when she offered her cut wrist again, he took it without hesitation.

Mira smiled inwardly, watching him feed from her arm. He might not be a warrior, but he certainly was a survivor. A do-whatever-it-takes kind of guy. That she could appreciate.

Sarah came down the stairs with a bucket of sanitizer water and towels. "I couldn't find any plastic bags to wrap them..." Her words cut off when she caught sight of Lucian feeding from Mira. "What the hell?"

"He was injured. This will help him heal fast," Mira explained simply. There was no time for making nice about it.

"Stop that this instant. Do you want to become like her?" she chided Lucian.

"Sarah, honey..." Curtis said.

"No. It's bad enough she got us into this mess. Now she's trying to change him."

"I assure you, that is not the case." Mira started to defend herself, but decided it was not worth her time. If a person hated her, there was nothing she could really do to stop them. Humans were often too short-sighted as it was.

"I want to be rid of you... the sooner the better." Her contempt was obvious, yet other than her words, she made no further attempt to push the matter.

"Me too," Mira agreed.

Sarah huffed and went to work cleaning

Lucian pulled away from Mira's offered wrist. He gagged and spat up some of the blood he'd drunk.

"Hold still," Mira ordered. "I need to make sure it's working."

She inspected the wound. The bleeding, thankfully, had slowed to a trickle. He'd heal soon enough, but that still left them with a problem. How were they going to get out together... and alive?

"Strip them down," Lucian said, indicating the fallen soldiers.

Mira arched an eyebrow suspiciously.

"Their uniforms are Kevlar. That will provide us with some additional protection we might need."

Smart idea. Mira nodded and went to work removing the clothes from the soldier she had just killed. His communicator bracer began to beep when she tried to unfasten it. "Sanders. Report," came a voice through the communicator's small speaker.

Mira looked to Lucian and attempted with only her eyes to ask him what to do. Her first instinct was to smash it, but she'd never been allowed close to any kind of modern technology and wasn't sure if it might be useful in some way.

The communicator beeped again. "Sanders, do you copy?"

Curtis stepped up and grabbed the dead soldier's arm, ripping the communicator off. He fiddled with the buttons on the communicator, but by the anxious look on his face, was not getting the result he wanted. Finally, after the third time the person on the other side called for Sanders, Curtis pulled a sharp tool from his workbench and stabbed at it a few times. Strange screeches and electric pops finally ended the communication.

"What did you do that for?" Mira asked.

"Assuming it had a tracking beacon, I'd say we bought ourselves a little time," Curtis responded.

"Right. Good thinking. How much longer until sunset?" Mira asked.

"Little more than an hour, I'd say." Curtis tossed his tool back on the workbench.

"Tracking beacon or not, they'll know the last location of that soldier before he went missing. I doubt we bought ourselves any additional time." Lucian's tone was somber. "Don't forget the other one. We'll need to disable his com-link as well."

"Aye," Curtis said, retrieving his tool, and headed over to the other dead soldier. "Then we'll have to leave sooner rather than later."

"Mira, how long can you be in sunlight?" Lucian asked.

"Direct light? Not long. Even if the light wasn't touching my skin, it would still affect my vision. Too much light is blinding."

"What about sunshields or lenses? That soldier might have had a helmet. Sarah, can you run out and check if they had a transport?"

Sarah looked up from her scrubbing and sneered at Mira, as if it were her fault she could not handle the sun. "Anything to be away from that." If glares could kill, Mira would have been six feet under by now.

Mira did her best to ignore Sarah. "A helmet with a sunshade might help in indirect light; not sure how much, though. It really depends on how much light it filters out."

"Well, it's better than nothing," Lucian said. "Curtis, do you have transport or a vehicle of any kind?"

"Sorry, sir, I'm not affluent enough to own anything like that."

"Do you have any friends who would let you borrow one?" Lucian asked.

"Not on short notice."

"On foot, through a city guarded by hundreds of soldiers looking to kill us. Sounds like a great time." Mira's voice dripped with sarcasm.

"Don't forget with a blind vampire too," Lucian added.

"That's the spirit." Hopeless as their situation was, Mira had to appreciate Lucian's attempt at a joke.

"No transport outside or nearby," Sarah called from the top of the stairs.

"That makes things difficult," Lucian sighed.

"Yeah, and no helmet either," Mira said.

"We'll just have to make do. Curtis, you have any sunglasses?" Lucian asked.

Curtis finished stripping down the soldier and tossed the clothes in a heap in front of Lucian. "I'm sure I can scrounge up a pair."

"Good. Please hurry," Lucian said. "Mira, you'll probably fit in the smaller uniform." He nudged the pile of heavy clothes toward her. "The boots will be big. Just try to make them work for now. We need to look as much of the part as we can."

"You have a plan beyond impersonating a soldier?"

"No. That's pretty much it. We just need to blend in for an hour or so until sunset. We can better do that in uniform, patrolling the streets, than running like a pair of fugitives, right?"

"Hide in plain sight, sure. It's simple enough it might just work." Mira was impressed, but skeptical. "But what do we do with the bodies? We can't leave them here. Curtis and Sarah will be implicated."

"They'll have to come with us. We'll escort them around under the guise of taking them back to central command."

Mira wanted to argue against bringing the other humans along. The longer they stayed together, the more danger they would be in. But she saw no other way around it. There was no time to properly dispose of the bodies, and two dead soldiers in their home, no matter the reason why, would be a death sentence for this couple.

Mira finished pulling on the soldier's uniform. It hung loosely on her shoulders and was baggy throughout. She hoped no one would pay too close attention, because she was obviously not a soldier.

Sarah came downstairs. "Here. Let me help with your hair." She grabbed some oil from Curtis's work bench and used it to slick back Mira's short dark hair. "This will make you look more like a man."

Surprised at the gesture, Mira's voice caught in her throat as she tried to thank the perplexing woman.

"Save your thanks," Sarah said with all the spite and vitriol she'd shown earlier. "I'm doing this as much for myself as I am for you."

That was more of what she expected. "I appreciate the honesty." Mira truly did. She understood the human's revulsion at her species, but the fact that she was not letting blind hatred color her actions earned some respect.

Sarah finished with Mira's hair and handed her a pair of large-lens sun glasses. "It's the best we've got here."

"It'll have to do."

Dressed and ready, Lucian cautiously opened the door and looked outside. In the distance sirens had started. The other soldiers were on their way.

Lucian looked back. "I'll take Sarah, you take Curtis," he said to Mira. "Make it look like you're taking them in for questioning. Like this." He grabbed hold of Sarah's upper arm and tugged her forward. "Walk slowly and keep your head down, okay?"

Sarah nodded.

Mira reached out cautiously to Curtis, more for his comfort than her own apprehension. He may have seemed comfortable around her, but it was wholly another thing to be in the clutches of a predator. "Why don't you take the lead? I'll be a bit blind, so you'll have to guide me."

Looking as if he were steeling his courage, Curtis nodded and held out his arm for Mira to hold.

"Let's move out," Lucian ordered. He held his gun in one hand, pointed toward Sarah, and guided her forward with his other hand around her arm.

Mira winced as she followed through the door. Even though the cloud cover was in her favor, the light filtering though her sunglasses from the overcast sky was still annoyingly bright. She paused at the threshold and took a breath, looking down to the ground to try to allow her eyes to adjust and focus.

"Are you going to be able to do this?" Curtis asked, sounding surprisingly concerned.

"I always do what I must to survive. It is the way of my people."

"Vampires?"

"Gladiators." She let the weight of the word sink in. "This light is harsh, but a full blast from a UV torch is a bit more powerful."

"Enough talk, let's move," Lucian called back from the street.

Mira didn't want to admit it, but there was something about the way he sounded, when giving orders, that really connected with her. "Go." She nodded stiffly and let Curtis set their pace.

Sirens were closer now. A block away, if Mira's guess was right. Unable to really see where they were going and what was around, Mira tried to recall what she'd seen on their run the previous night. "We need to find a way off the main roads. What's behind these rowhouses?"

"There's an alleyway for trash collection and utilities," Curtis responded.

"Utilities... what about sewer?"

"Nowhere to access the tunnels back there, if that's what you're after. You'd be better off finding a street hatch."

"If we can get off high traffic roads and locate one, we might just have a way out," Mira said.

A large armored vehicle pulled up alongside of the road, its siren blaring.

"You there," a soldier called out from the passenger window. "What are you doing?"

Lucian stepped forward pulling Sarah roughly with him and pulled his sidearm. He pressed the gun to Sarah's side. "Caught these two escaping from a house about a block over."

The soldier pulled up an address on his dash-mounted screen. "2857 Stonebend?"

"That's the one. But I wouldn't get too close. This one here rigged some kind of EMP." Lucian lifted his arm, showing off his non-functioning bracer. "Knocked out our com-links. Couldn't radio in. We're going to take these two in to command."

"Need a lift?"

"Nah. There are two dead bodies in the basement of that old house. Someone's going to have to get in there and get a cleanup crew going. Why don't you radio that in? Word is they were harboring the fugitives. I'd say they made a break for it and are probably roaming the streets as we speak."

"Roger that."

"Let them know we're coming in on foot with two prisoners, too," Lucian added.

As the large transport began to pull away, Mira breathed a sigh of relief. That had gone more smoothly than she could have hoped for. And Lucian, the way he talked, with such command – his Elite side was definitely showing through. She began to think they might actually pull this off.

They continued on, Mira moving slowly behind, concentrating on every step, the light burning her eyes. The sound of tires screeching caught her attention. Then a shot was fired from behind. She turned and tried to focus on the transport. Either it was growing larger, or it was heading back in her direction.

"Shit! Time for plan B. Get down!" Mira shouted.

The transport came to a screeching halt next to them. Three soldiers inside had guns trained on them. "On second thought. Why don't you all come quietly with us?" One of the soldiers slid open the side door. Still pointing his gun, he nodded at Lucian. "You and the girl first."

"Ladies always go first." Using a burst of her supernatural speed, Mira jumped the soldier and in one smooth motion snapped his neck. One of the other soldiers in the vehicle shot at her blindly. She felt the sting of the heated metal piercing her flesh, but would not let it deter her from her mission. She snapped the driver's neck and then ripped away the gun from the last soldier. "Oh, I'm going to enjoy this." She lunged at him, ripping away his Kevlar body armor like tissue paper, and sank her teeth into his tender flesh.

"Now we have transportation to get us where we need. I say we take this baby and ram it through the front gates." Flushed full of adrenaline-soaked blood, Mira was ready for another fight. She felt like she could take on all the soldiers in the city.

"We'll do that... but on a smaller scale," Lucian replied. "I know every entrance and exit in the city. We'll want to hit the least likely one to bring attention. One only Elites are allowed to use." He winked and took the driver seat. "Get in, you two," he called back to Curtis and Sarah.

The sweet coppery tang of blood caught Mira's attention. More than there should be in the air. She looked back to find the horrified, struggling Sarah trying her best to lift Curtis off the ground. Blood pooled beneath his body. His face had gone dangerously pale.

Mira jumped out of the car and helped Sarah lift him. The scent of his freshly spilled blood tempted her, especially being so close to it. She could lap it up off the ground and enjoy every last drop, but her concern for their situation and the urgency of their need to move kept her riveted to the task at hand. "Get him inside. I'll try my best to heal him."

Curtis moaned weakly, barely audible even with Mira's enhanced hearing, as they pulled him inside the vehicle. This didn't look good. Mira feared he might be too far gone. The desperation in Sarah's eyes made that thought ten times worse. They were the ones risking their human, mortal lives for her, a slave.

No, she couldn't let him die. Mira ripped open Curtis's shirt to inspect his wound.

"What are we waiting for? Drive!" Mira shouted to Lucian.

"Where to?"

"Anywhere, just get us out of here now."

Lucian put the vehicle into gear. It lurched forward, and Mira turned her attention to Curtis.

"Will he be all right?" Sarah was frantic. She hovered over her husband.

Mira tried to push her back. "I'll give him my blood. It should help jumpstart his body's natural healing."

"Should?"

Mira didn't have to look up to know the fright that would be written all over Sarah's face. She did her best to give her an honest reply, though, not wanting to deliver false hope, but not wanting to scare her further. "It's not an exact science. It really depends on how much blood he's lost, and how bad the wounds are. I don't know if the bullet is still in his body or not."

"Just help him!" Sarah demanded.

Mira ripped open her wrist and held it to Curtis's mouth. Moments before, when she had done this to help Lucian, Sarah had practically condemned her; but now that the tables were turned, she didn't care what happened. Sarah just wanted her husband to be okay.

Curtis wasn't swallowing. His breathing was deathly shallow. Mira massaged his throat to help encourage him to swallow as his mouth filled with her blood.

With her free hand she prodded the wound, inspecting it but also hoping to get a response from Curtis. Anything, even a pain response would be good at this moment. He was too close to death, and Mira desperately wanted to see him live.

The bullet must have passed through her and hit him in the chest. She guessed it still remained. Depending on how far gone he was, her blood might not make any difference at all. If the bullet had hit a vital organ, there might be no hope. The good news – if you could call it that – was that there was blood on Curtis's back as well. If the bullet had passed directly through him, it might be his saving grace. If she could get the bastard to swallow. This man had risked everything to save her and Lucian. He did not deserve this as his fate.

"Drink, damn you!" She slammed a fist against his chest. "Wake up and drink!"

"Stop that, you'll hurt him!" Sarah shrieked.

"Do you know CPR?" Mira asked.

"Yes. Do you want me to do chest compressions?"

Mira listened for a moment for the sounds of his breathing, and the faint thump of his heart. Even with her enhanced hearing, both were scarcely audible. "His heart is barely beating…. Yes."

"But your blood is supposed to heal him!" Panic stole Sarah's voice.

"It will…. One way or another," Mira said somberly.

"What's that supposed to mean?" Sarah shot back at her angrily.

"I'm trying to save him—"

"You're not trying hard enough. Do you even want to save him?"

Mira had to rein in her annoyance. Sarah's husband was on the brink of death; it was understandable for her to be a little snippy. At least, that's what she told herself to avoid snapping the human's neck for daring to challenge her.

"Just start pumping his chest," she said through clenched teeth.

She reopened the wound that had closed in her wrist and again flooded Curtis's mouth with her blood. "Drink, you bastard!" She rubbed his Adam's apple and massaged his throat while Sarah went to work thrusting hard on his chest. Curtis's rib cracked under the pressure, and Sarah jumped back off him.

"That's normal, and my blood will heal the broken rib. Just keep up compressions. I need his blood pumping, no matter how slow."

Thankfully, Sarah did not argue this time. Steel-faced, she went back to her task, pumping hard at her husband's chest.

Mira was beginning to lose hope, until finally, Curtis swallowed on his own. She ripped open the wound again at her wrist and forced it hard down on his mouth. "That's it. Drink up!"

Sarah must have understood the relief in Mira's voice. She relaxed her arms and stopped pressing on his chest. "C'mon, my darling." The sensitivity in her voice touched Mira on a level she hadn't known in a long time. This was love. Something she had long been denied, but was still alive in this world.

Curtis swallowed on his own; and again. Slowly, color came back to his cheeks. He groaned and tried to lift his arms.

"Easy there, friend. You're not out of the woods yet," Mira cautioned.

"You did it!" Sarah practically squealed with delight as she flung herself on top of Curtis, squeezing him tightly against her.

Mira let out a small sigh. "He appears to be conscious, but I wouldn't say he's saved yet. I need to get a better look at his wounds, make sure they are healing."

Curtis tried to move again and winced in pain.

"Don't try to be the tough guy here. Just relax," Mira cautioned again, and placed a firm hand on his shoulder to emphasize her point.

"Look sharp, people," Lucian called from the driver seat. "The city gates are up ahead. We're going to need some help up here."

"He's going to be fine," Mira said to Sarah. "I can't do any more for him now."

"You've done enough. Now, go see what Lucian needs."

Mira smiled at the human ordering her around. "Yes, Ma'am," she said playfully, and then turned and headed up to the driver's seat. "What's the situation?"

One hand on the wheel, Lucian pointed straight ahead with the other. "There are a few more soldiers guarding the gate than I had anticipated."

Mira stood and peered out of the front windshield. The sun hadn't quite set yet, but was low enough in the horizon to be blocked by taller buildings. Ahead, she spotted a large blockade. Four tank-like vehicles, similar to the one they were driving, flanked a narrow gated road. Armed soldiers stood in front of the gate, weapons raised and ready to shoot.

"This thing have any weaponry?" Mira asked.

"Roof-mounted gun, I believe."

Mira looked up and spotted a roof hatch above where Sarah and Curtis were sitting. She didn't want to have to expose herself, but there was no other way. She could take a few gunshots better than the humans. Before anyone could utter another word, she flipped open the hatch and took to the roof.

No words were needed; Lucian and Mira were on the same wavelength. There was no way to get through the blockade except straight ahead, at full speed. Lucian pressed the accelerator as Mira began to fire blindly at the soldiers blocking their path.

She barely felt the first few bullets pierce her skin – it was the sting of sun's bright light, even at this late hour, that had Mira gritting her teeth to stop the scream from tearing up her throat. She focused all of her energy on enduring and keeping her weapon firing as they barreled through the road blocks and rolled over bodies in the street.

They smashed through the gate with ease, Mira ducking down to avoid the flying splinters of wood as they continued through.

Even with the city walls behind them, Mira could still hear shots being fired and the shouting of soldiers. The rumble of tanks told her, without having to look, that this fight was far from over.

Mira ducked her head down into the vehicle. "Can we outrun them?"

"In the city, we could out-maneuver them; on the open road, doubtful." Lucian sounded worried.

"Do what you can, then. I'll try my best to hold them off."

She resumed her place, swiveling the gun around, pointing at what she hoped was the tanks behind them. The sun's light was still too bright to allow her to focus well enough to be sure.

She fired off a few rounds, but heard no sound of ricochet. In return, a pursuing tank fired, narrowly missing her. The sound of the racing bullet broke the air next to her cheek. A few inches to the left and she might have been done for. She could well be immortal, but that did not make her invincible. "I need some eyes here," Mira shouted. "I can't see a damn thing."

Another shot whizzed past her head, parting her hair. "Now!" she screamed, and fired back blindly at the vehicle behind her.

Sarah's head popped up next to her. "Left," she called.

Mira inched the barrel of the gun over to the left and fired another shot.

"Down just a hair," Sarah instructed.

Mira moved accordingly and fired again. This time she was rewarded by the sound of breaking glass.

"Now, quick right," Sarah instructed again.

Mira adjusted and fired. Again she heard her shots connect, this time clanging off metal. "Did I get one?"

"We knocked one of them off course for the moment. Broken windshield. But you still have another one on our tail. Move to the left again."

The vehicle behind fired. Sarah ducked down, pulling Mira with her. Bullets whizzed past again.

"They're still right on us!" Lucian shouted.

"I'm working on it," Mira snapped back at him. She stood again, taking hold of the gun and blasting off a few more blind rounds at the vehicles behind her.

Sarah stood with her and directed again. Together they worked, slowly aiming and adjusting until one of Mira's bullets actually hit a human target. She wasn't able to see it, but she heard the moaning yelp as a bullet took out one of the soldiers.

The sun was sinking lower, and Mira was starting to be able to make out her targets. She aimed to take out the windshield of the vehicle directly behind them. A few well-placed shots shattered the thick glass enough to prevent the driver from seeing. They were forced off course, leaving only one vehicle in pursuit. This one appeared to be lacking a gunman. Its window smashed, Mira looked for the right spot to shoot.

"Slow it down just a bit," she called back to Lucian.

The vehicle slowed and the pursuing soldiers quickly gained on them. Mira squinted, aiming her gun carefully. She squeezed off a few shots, missing her target. They slowed and backed off, cutting across to the other side of their vehicle.

"Damn the sun!" Mira cursed for missing such an easy shot. "Hit the brakes, make them catch up again," she called back to her driver.

This time she would not fail. She took aim, watching, adjusting as the other vehicle came suddenly closer. When they were directly behind again, she fired.

This time her shot hit the mark. The other vehicle came to a dead stop.

"That's it, gun it!" she called back to Lucian. "We're in the clear. Drive."

Breathing a well-earned sigh of relief, Mira ducked back into the cabin of her transport. "We did it."

"Great. Now what?" Lucian's hands gripped the steering wheel so tightly Mira wondered if he might break it off.

"What do you mean, now what?" Mira asked. "We're in the clear. You can relax a bit."

"Where do we go from here?" Lucian wasn't letting his guard down that easy. White-knuckled, he continued to stare straight ahead and left his foot planted on the pedal of the vehicle.

Good question… Mira wasn't exactly sure. "Just keep driving west for now, I guess." She'd never actually made it to the safe haven. Never knew its exact location either, only that it was off the coast in the badlands once known as California. If it didn't exist, they were on yet another fool's errand; but if it did, she might actually finally get the freedom she so truly desired. Then, she'd work on a way to end the Magistrate and share that precious freedom with her other imprisoned friends.

So much was riding on this, she almost dared not hope that it truly existed.

NEXT IN THE CHRONICLES OF
THE UPRISING

COMPLICATION

Narrowly escaping death at the hands of the Magistrate, Mira travels west, toward the coast. With three weakened human fugitives accompanying her, she searches for the mythical land of Sanctuary.

After encountering a pack of wolf shifters, headed by the charismatic—and brazen—Stryker, Mira learns that Sanctuary is real after all. Caldera Grove: home of the Otherkin. Hidden in the mouth of a dormant volcano, it has protected its residents from humans since the early days following the great cataclysm. For Mira— a vampire— Caldera Grove is a land of peace; an escape from the relentless persecution of the humans who once enslaved her, and an end to the daily struggle and bloodshed of being a gladiator.

For the humans accompanying her, Caldera Grove means death. Humans, greedy and untrustworthy creatures, are destroyed before they can penetrate its borders.

To plead her case for entry into Caldera, Mira must abandon her companions, albeit temporarily, and follow Stryker into the heart of the city. What she finds within Caldera Grove presents her with an unenviable decision between her own desires for freedom and peace, or honor and the human companions who risked it all for her.

COMPLICATION

Sample Chapter 1

Thousands of twinkling stars lit the night sky above, a glorious sight Mira had not seen in more years than she could count. Their majesty stole the breath from her chest. Night called her like a siren's song both familiar and strange. Imprisoned deep under the ground as she'd been all those long years, not even allowed to smell the crispness of night air, the melody had long since been forgotten but never truly lost. More than a delicacy, it called forth primal urges, reaching some long-repressed savage part of her. It was all Mira could do not to pull the vehicle over and take off into the wild, but the trio of humans riding along with her, escaping to safety, needed her to remain on task.

Eyes riveted to the rugged landscape behind them, Mira screened the horizon for any signs of pursuit. The badlands—a mix of ruined forest and parched hard-packed dirt—stretched out as far as the eye could see. Regular monsoon flooding had made the land tough and treacherous. Their transport, not equipped for off-roading, jolted and rocked, banged and bumped as it sped on between gnarled trees and mountainous boulders.

Hours had passed since their daring escape from New Haven city behind the Iron Gate walls, one of the eight human city-states and the westernmost point of the Northern continent. Though there had been no sign of their vehicle being followed, Mira was not yet ready to stop for a break. She had no clue of the capability and reach of the humans beyond their city walls. The last thing she wanted was to give in to fatigue too soon and end up right back where she started... in prison.

Painful memories drove her to her task. Thirty long years she'd been enslaved; thirty years of torture, pain, violence, and bloodshed... all of it under the orders of her human masters. Olivia's face flashed through her mind. Her former owner. If she'd only had the opportunity to pay the pampered princess back for the vile things she'd had endured. The things she'd been forced to do. Countless vampires she'd been forced to kill. Cold dead eyes of numerous victims haunted her dreams, and probably would for the rest of her immortal life.

Killing had been her way of life. Survival. Kill or be killed. As a gladiator, there was no middle ground. In the arena, by order of her masters, she'd sent so many others to early graves. It was enough to make her hungry for revenge on all members of the so-called human race. The lot of them were untrustworthy, greedy, vengeful, lying bastards.

Mira shot a heated glance toward Lucian. Human. Former Regent. One who had, in the past, ordered the death of many of her kind. At a single turn of his thumb she herself had been forced to end the lives of many vampire kin, ripping out their throats while crowds cheered above her.

And they called *her* a savage. Mira scoffed at the irony.

She should hate Lucian as much as she hated the rest of human society; she certainly had the right to. But not all humans were bad. At least not that one, she reminded herself as her gaze narrowed down his short dark hair toward the crook of his neck, spotting the pulsating artery there. It would be so easy to sink her fangs in and drink her fill. Lucian had once been part of the problem, but no longer. He'd helped save her from her imprisonment. He'd proven his true nature. She looked back to the other two humans in the vehicle – the aging Curtis and his wife, Sarah, huddling together, fighting exhaustion. They too had helped, despite obvious revulsion at her species. Not all humans were the enemy. Not all were evil. Just as she, a vampire, was not evil.

She dragged in another breath of that glorious fresh night air and let it clear away the anger. So many years she had dreamed of freedom, and now she had it.

She was free. Alive. No more silver shackles. No more tiny cell smelling of dirt and decay. No more fighting for her life in the arena. Sure, they were still in danger, and the humans would certainly pursue her, but in this one moment, she was free. The crispness of that single breath stirred within her the desire for more. Others too should savor this freedom. She thought back to the prison and all of the vampires still trapped within. George, the closest thing she'd had to a true friend. Tegan, her last opponent. He'd been her enemy in the arena and in training, but he didn't deserve to remain locked behind silver-coated bars. Countless others were still languishing away within the Iron Gate prison. Those poor souls. They needed to know that there was more to immortality than servitude.

"You okay, Mira?" Lucian's weary tone was soft as a whisper.

Quiet as they were, his words snapped Mira from her thoughts. "Yeah. Why?"

"You just look…" Lucian hesitated as if unable to complete the thought.

"I'm fine. I just haven't seen the stars in so long. They're so beautiful."

Lucian glanced upwards, but his eyes didn't sparkle the way Mira had hoped. "I guess."

"Don't take them for granted. You don't know what it's like to miss them."

"I can only imagine." He forced a smile.

She couldn't be too annoyed with him. Living a life of privilege, as he had, wanting for nothing, how could she expect him to appreciate something as small yet significant as the stars shimmering in the night sky? There was a time when she too had taken them for granted. "Nice driving back there." She hoped the subject change would break the awkward silence between them.

His chest puffed with pride. "I have to admit, it was pretty exciting."

Mira smiled at the sudden change in his demeanor. She doubted he'd ever experienced anything as thrilling as their escape in his life. "I'll be honest. I had my doubts we'd make it."

"Really?" His shoulders slumped slightly.

"Three humans and one half-blind vampire being chased by trained soldiers? Think about it. The odds weren't exactly in our favor, now, were they?"

"You should give us more credit than that."

"We did it. We survived and we're still alive. That's credit enough. Don't get cocky; you'll become sloppy." She didn't mean to downplay their abilities, but being a realist, she wouldn't sugarcoat things. That wasn't the warrior way.

Lucian's jaw tightened. Clearly dissatisfied by her lack of praise, he turned away, looking out the window toward the horizon. "So, do you have an idea as to where we're going?"

"No." Sanctuary had always been a land of legend. A rumor spread among the vampires wanting to find freedom from oppression. She'd been on the road to finding it once; before she'd been captured. Back when she was just a fledgling traveling with her sire and lover, Theo. All she remembered from those days was that they'd been heading west, toward the coast. "Nor do I know what we'll do or find if we ever get there."

"Well, you're just a bright little ray of sunshine tonight, aren't you?"

"I don't like sunshine, and I'm not going to pretend we're in the clear. We've still got a lot of question marks hanging above our heads."

"We've overcome quite a lot tonight. Allow yourself to accept that."

He was right. She glanced back up to the stars for a moment and let their silvery light brighten her mood. "I'm just concerned about what we have coming up next. Good or bad."

Lucian gently squeezed Mira's arm, a small gesture of friendship and camaraderie that felt so foreign. Touching was not something she was used to, and not something she was too sure she liked.

"I've been thinking about that as well," Lucian said. "Assuming we make it, we'll be in vampire territory. You'll have to take the lead."

"One thing at a time. First we have to find it." Mira hadn't thought about what would happen when they did encounter other vampires. She'd be reasonably safe on her own, but with three humans in tow, she was traveling with her own personal buffet. Her own kind back home had become near savage over the years in captivity; what would free-range vampires be like? What did they feed on? Assuming they had survived, what had they lived off all of these long years? So many questions. So many new worries. In some respects, this newfound freedom promised to be just as problematic as captivity.

"When we do find it, we'll need to have a plan in place."

Mira took a deep breath and gazed back up at the stars, trying to use their light to help her remain positive. "Can we leave the future to the future for now? I've not seen the stars in so long. I want to enjoy this simple pleasure for the moment."

"The stars will always be there."

"Says the man who's had a lifetime to enjoy them."

Lucian sighed impatiently but did not engage her further. They rode together in silence, putting more and more miles between themselves and New Haven's Iron Gate.

OTHER TITLES BY KATIE SALIDAS

The Immortalis Series:

Becoming a vampire is easy. Living with the condition... that's the hard part. Join Alyssa as she stumbles through the world of the "Unnatural."

Book 1: Immortalis Carpe Noctem - Newbie vampire Alyssa never asked for this life, but now it's all she has. Rescued from death by Lysander, the aloof and sexy leader of the Peregrinus vampire clan, she's barely cut her teeth before she becomes a target. Kallisto, an ancient and vindictive vampire queen – and Lysander's old mate - wants nothing less than final death for her former lover and his new toy. She's not above letting the Acta Sanctorum, and its greatest vampire hunter, Santino, know exactly where the clan can be found.With no time to mourn her old life, Alyssa's survival depends on her new family. She will have to stand alongside Lysander and fight against two enemies who will stop at nothing to destroy them.

Book 2: Hunters & Prey - Rule number one: humans and vampires don't co-exist. One is the hunter and one is the prey. Simple, right? Not for newly-turned vampire Alyssa. A surprise confrontation with Santino Vitale, the Acta Sanctorum's most fearsome hunter, sends her fleeing back to the world she once knew, and Fallon, the human friend she's missed more than anything. Now she has some explaining to do. However, that will have to wait. With the Acta Sanctorum hot on their heels, staying alive is more important than educating a human on the finer points of bloodlust.

Book 3: Pandora's Box - After a few months as a vampire, Alyssa thought she'd learned all she needed to know about the supernatural world. But her confidence is shattered by the delivery of a mysterious package - a Pandora's Box. Seemingly innocuous, the box is in reality an ancient prison, generated by a magic more powerful than anyone in her clan has ever known. But what manner of evil could need such force to contain it? When the box is opened, the sinister creature within is released, and only supernatural blood will satiate its thirst. The clan soon learns how it feels when the hunter becomes the hunted.

Book 4: Soulstone - It's a desperate time for rookie vampire Alyssa, and her sanity is hanging by a slender thread. Her clan is still reeling from the monumental battle with Aniketos; a battle that claimed the body of Lysander, her sire and lover, and trapped his spirit in a mysterious crystal. A Soulstone. Unfortunately, no amount of magic has been able to release Lysander's spirit, and the stone is starting to fade. Weeks of effort have proved futile. Her clan, the Peregrinus, have all but given up hope. Only Alyssa still believes her lover can be released. In despair, Alyssa begs the help of the local witch coven, and unwittingly exposes the supernaturals of Boston to unwanted attention from the Acta Sanctorum. The Saints converge on the city and begin their cleansing crusade to rid the world of all things "Unnatural." In the middle of an all-out war, but no closer to a solution to the dying stone, Alyssa is left with an unenviable choice: save her mate, or save her clan.

Book 5: Moonlight

Good girls don't wear fur, or fight over men, and they certainly don't run around naked, howling at the moon. But then, no-one ever called Fallon a good girl. As a human *unofficially* mated to an Alpha werewolf, Fallon is being pressured to "become"...or be gone. Her mate Aiden, the interim leader of the Olde Town Pack, is in a position that demands he either choose a wolf mate...or leave the pack forever. No matter how hot the sex with Fallon is, he can't ignore centuries of tradition. Become a wolf or not. If only the choice were that simple. Fallon's options are further clouded by the overt presence of other females desperate to be the Alpha's mate. And when these bitches get serious, it's not just claws that come out. If Fallon wants to keep her man and take the title she'll have to exert a little dominance of her own.

Book 6: Dark Salvation

A gathering storm of violence is on the horizon. Whispered threats of the Acta Sanctorum's return have the supernatural world abuzz. Only recently aware of the other world hidden behind our own, Kitara Vanders has barely scratched the surface of what being supernatural truly means. A special woman in her own right, she possesses unique telepathic abilities, gifts that have recently come under the scrutiny of the Acta Sanctorum, a fanatical organization whose mission is to cleanse the world of anything supernatural. Targeted, and marked for death, Kitara's only hope lies with the lethally seductive yet emotionally scarred warrior, Nicholas.

Knowing full well the atrocities the Acta Sanctorum is capable of, Nicholas is all too eager for the battle to begin. Fueled by pain and rage from the loss of his mate, he's itching for a fight, but one thing stands in his way, Kitara: a beautiful dark-haired woman with unique psychic abilities and an unusual link to the Saints. Despite his resolve to remain focused on his mission, a purely physical relationship binds them together in a way neither of them expected. And when her life hangs in the balance, Nicholas finds his own is teetering on the edge too.

ABOUT THE AUTHOR

Katie Salidas is a Super Woman! Endowed with special powers and abilities, beyond those of mortal women, She can get the munchkin off to gymnastics, cheerleading, Girl Scouts, and swim lessons. She can put hot food on the table for dinner while assisting with homework, baths, and bedtime... And, She still finds the time to keep the hubby happy (nudge nudge wink wink). She can do all of this and still have time to write.

And if you can believe all of those lies, there is some beautiful swamp land in Florida for sale...

Katie Salidas resides in Las Vegas, Nevada. Mother, wife, and author, she does try to do it all, often causing sleep deprivation and many nights passed out at the computer. Writing books is her passion, and she hopes that her passion will bring you hours of entertainment.

Find Katie Salidas online at:

http://www.katiesalidas.com/

Facebook
http://www.facebook.com/pages/Katie-Salidas-Author/214780936916

LinkedIn
http://www.linkedin.com/profile?viewProfile=&key=58814031&trk=tab_pro

Twitter
http://twitter.com/QuixoticKatie